Perfect SEDUCTION

MIA LONDON

Perfect Seduction

by Mia London

This is a work of fiction. Names, characters, places and incidents either are the product of the author's imagination or are used factitiously, and any resemblance to actual persons, living or dead, business establishments, event or locales is entirely coincidental.

ISBN 978-0-9905274-4-2

Publisher: Mia London
PO Box 93852
Southlake, TX 76092

Cover photo by Shutterstock.

Cover design by JLH Designs.

ACKNOWLEDGEMENTS:

To Rossie, thank you for making me a better writer.

To Leti, Beth and Diane, thank you for being my NYC experts.

To Alla, because everyone should have an actress as a friend.

To all my dear friends and family for their support, encouragement and great ideas. I couldn't have done it without you.

CHAPTER ONE

"COLE, ARE YOU home?" Lauren called from the front door of their Soho apartment.

Cole appeared around the corner carrying a longneck beer. "What's up, sis?"

"You are not going to believe the call I got today." She spoke fast, her eyes ablaze. She walked to the kitchen table, set down her purse and sunglasses. She pulled out a chair and sat. Cole joined her.

"Tell me." He leaned back intrigued.

She faced him, her voice now sober. "I got a call from a lawyer in Paris. Aunt Rosie died."

"Who?" Cole squinted his eyes.

"Mom's only sister. You may not remember her. She lived in the States for a while, then moved to Paris years ago."

Looking off to the side, he said, "Ya' know, I do vaguely remember her at Mom and Dad's funeral." Of course, a six-year-old boy can't be expected to remember much from such a traumatic day. He brought his focus back to his sister. "How sad. What happened?"

"According to the lawyer, she died with a smile on her face." A small smile graced her pretty face. Lauren described what a daredevil Aunt Rosie was.

"Anyway, she left her estate to us. Apparently, the value is about three million dollars!"

"Holy cow!" Cole's eyes rounded.

"I know. Here's the kicker. I have to go to Paris to settle everything—the sooner, the better."

"Okay. Great. What are you going to do about work? Do you think Witch Regina will give you the time off?"

Regina Skorpio was the Leona Helmsley of the spa industry. She was hard as nails, rude, unyielding and driven by the almighty dollar.

"Well, . . . that's why I wanted to talk to you first. I expect to be gone for a month. Although I have the vacation time, Regina certainly wouldn't let me take it all at once. So I have an idea," she said with a hint of playful wickedness.

"Yeah?"

"If I go to Regina with a 'stand-in' she should be okay. Someone I can convince her would provide a seamless transition."

"Okay, that could work. Who did you have in mind? Gretchen? Andrea?"

"No. Gretchen has too many edges and Andrea's too indecisive. Actually, the person I have in mind is congenial, organized, trustworthy and a multi-tasker," she said pulling him into her plan.

Cole raised his eyebrows waiting to hear her solution.

"You."

He almost choked on his beer at her comment. "No freaking way, Lauren."

"Yes, Cole, think about it," she said with pleading eyes. "You know the business. You know most of the clientele. You know the girls and their personalities. That's what we do—talk about work, right? I could drop you in there tomorrow, and the spa wouldn't miss a beat. You can do this."

"Sis, you are flippin' out of your mind. I don't know the services, the systems, and have you forgotten—I'd be the only male in a clothing-optional spa," his voice rose decibels to practically yelling. His sister was off her ever-loving rocker. Cole stood up, feeling more than a little agitated by Lauren's preposterous suggestion.

"Well, I've thought of that. There is one way the clientele wouldn't care less if you worked there—"

"And saw them naked," he interrupted.

She nodded calmly. "And saw them naked . . . if you were gay."

"What? What the hell!"

"Hear me out, Cole. You know everything important about running L'Eclisse. Gretchen and Andrea can run the systems and close out the computers every night. I can make the schedule a month in advance. Regina won't care if it means she doesn't lose one drop of business. You just flatter the women, and they'll love you for being your usual charming self." She gave him a hesitant smile.

"I'll say it again—you have lost your mind. I am not going to act gay just to save your job." He stood to walk away from his sister and her ridiculous idea.

"Would you act gay for one and a half million bucks?" she raised her eyebrows at him.

That stopped Cole flat. His eyes went cold. "That's not fair."

"Cole, I'm not throwing accusations. All I'm saying is that I have to be there for a measly four weeks, and we inherit three million dollars. Work for you is slow during the summer, so stepping in for me right now would be perfect," she gestured with her hands out nonchalantly.

"I don't know, sis. Geez, what a flippin' crazy idea," he muttered as he went to the fridge for another beer.

"Just think about it, would you, Cole?" she pleaded.

***

Cole reached for his phone to call Ace on his way to meet his workers at a remodel job in the Upper West Side. He needed his friend's feedback on Lauren's idea about managing a female-only spa. He rolled his eyes.

"Dude, you're gonna have to give up your Man Card." Ace chuckled.

Cole growled. "It would only be for four weeks. I just gotta hang low for four weeks."

"So you're seriously thinking about this?"

"I don't know. I guess so. Remodeling is sometimes slow in the summer, and if I can help save my sister's job, I suppose it's worth it. Not to mention, according to my aunt's attorney there's three million bucks between us to share."

"No shit!"

"No shit."

"Man, you gotta do this."

Cole let out a long sigh of exasperation. "I don't know."

"Look, for one and a half million dollars, I'd wear a damn skirt," Ace said adamantly.

He chuckled at his friend's unique way of boiling it all down for him. "Okay, but what about the guys? I don't need them hanging around and blabbing the truth."

"Don't worry about it. They're all doing the ball-n-chain thing now, with the exception of Tim, who's in Delaware for a three-month consulting gig. I think you should be able to avoid them for four weeks."

"Alright." What else did he need to consider? "Any reason you see that I can't or shouldn't do this?" he asked in a resigned way.

"Nope. In fact, if I were in your shoes, I'd do the same damn thing."

"Shit. I thought you'd say that."

And Ace chuckled in his ear again. Cole had a feeling he'd be hearing a lot of that in the coming weeks.

That night Lauren brought home Chinese, and they talked more about her plan. Her insane plan. He'd mentioned to his crew that he had a project that would make him less visible for a while, but definitely still reachable. His company had a few client projects to finish up, but nothing new was on the horizon.

The last piece to the puzzle was Lauren's boss and Cole's "soon-to-be" boss.

"So, what did Regina say when you told her about me?"

"Ah," she smiled, "that was an interesting conversation, as I suspected it would be."

"How so?" he asked with a quizzical look on his face.

"Well, at first she was livid that I would consider leaving her stranded for four weeks. When I told her I had a gay brother who was more than capable of filling in for me, she went deathly quiet," Lauren said with her eyebrows raised. "I really thought it was the calm before the storm." She speared a piece of teriyaki beef from her dish.

Cole held his fork, anxiously waiting to hear the rest of the story. "And?"

"Well, turns out she was thinking it over. She never had a male work at her spa before, and she thought there was a chance it could work. Then she went on to drill me about my plans for getting you acclimated and introducing you to the clientele. She made me swear it wouldn't affect business. And..." she smiled a big fake smile to Cole, "she looked me square in the eyes, pointed a finger at my face and said 'Don't fuck this up, Knight, or your ass is toast.'"

Cole groaned. "She's so supportive," he murmured before taking a bite of *moo shu* pork.

"Well, at least she agreed. And I can't thank you enough Cole," she said grinning from ear to ear.

"I got this, sista. It'll be fantastic," he said adding a lilt to his voice.

She chuckled, and he shot her a smile. He'd do just about anything for Lauren. She was everything to him. Still, he was more confident on the outside than he felt on the inside.

CHAPTER TWO

"CUT!" THE DIRECTOR yelled and a moan carried across the set. Everyone was exhausted, including Alex.

Alexandra Marshall loved acting and dreamed about it since she was three. Now at twenty-seven she was rethinking her damned blessed dream.

"That's a wrap, people. See you tomorrow bright and early," the director called out to the cast spread around the props, walls, and floor.

"This is the latest they've kept us here," Gloria murmured to Alex as she gulped her water.

"Uh-huh. They might as well have cots brought in."

Gloria chuckled at her friend and fellow actor. They both had small parts in a big Hollywood movie, but both women needed the money, so any work was good work.

They gathered their belongings and trekked to the door. Gloria took the late bus, so she walked out the north exit of the building. Alex took the west exit.

Alex made the walk to her apartment since it wasn't very far from the studio. At this time of night—almost morning—the streets held just a handful of pedestrians. A few fellow actors headed the other way; a couple walked hand-in-hand on the opposite side of the street; a working girl stood against the brick wall waiting for a John. A car whooshed by. This part of town wasn't known to be the safest, so Alex reached into her purse to get her hands on her pepper spray.

She proceeded briskly passing a bum taking a snooze. Another car passed, rap music blaring through the open windows. She turned a corner, three blocks from her apartment. She saw no one and breathed a sigh of relief.

She made this walk a hundred times before, yet that night Alex was on edge. Perhaps because it was later than usual. She kept scanning the street. Not a soul in sight. She could see the entrance of her apartment two blocks up, when someone suddenly came up behind her, mere feet away. She glanced back. Where did he come from?

Alex's heart raced. She quickened her pace and heard the man's steps match hers. Shit! And without a moment to think or breathe, the man grabbed her arm and flung her face-first into the wall. The pepper spray fell from her hand, dangling from her wrist strap. She yelped in shock and pain.

His god-awful breath, passed over her ear, and he said in a low tone, "Give me your purse, your watch, and ring." He flashed a knife in front of her face.

She whimpered.

"Now," he uttered in a low and fierce tone.

Give him what he wants, and he'll go away.

He pushed her against the wall, the brick making imprints on her cheek, her attacker wasn't backing down. She slowly brought her right hand up to reach for the watch and her ring on her left hand.

Oh God, her ring. Her parents had given it to her as a graduation present from college. If only the pepper spray weren't hanging so damn low on her arm, she could have reached for it and sprayed his cold, evil eyes. Tears streamed down her face.

He grabbed her watch, ring, and purse, but didn't go. "Hmm, aren't you a nice piece of ass." Keeping one hand on her back pushing against it, he brought the other hand down to graze the knife over her ass.

She felt the tip of the knife through her pants smooth over one globe then the other. *Oh, God, no. Lord help me, please.*

Tears streamed unceasingly down her cheeks. Her heart raced. She couldn't breathe. Stay calm, she thought.

"Please, stop. I gave you what you wanted. Just go."

"I want something else," he whispered in her ear.

He took a hold of her waistband and yanked back. She squealed. "Make another sound, bitch, and I'll kill you."

As he kept a hand pushing against her back, she felt the knife glide down her low back into her pants and start to cut.

She whimpered and silently cried. *God, no.* She trembled as he proceeded with his sharp knife down the backside of her twill pants splitting them open. He started to tug on one pant leg, then the other pulling them down her thighs.

She froze in fear. She should fight. She had to fight, or she'd be raped. Or worse.

He brought the knife up to the waistband of her panties starting to shred them when someone from the street yelled, "Hey! Hey, you! What's going on!"

The man in the street started down toward them gaining speed as he got closer. Her assailant took off running in the opposite direction.

Alex couldn't move. She cried aloud and trembled from the fear that built inside her. She peeled off the wall as the man approached, and yanked up her split pants, trying to cover herself.

"Are you alright?" the man asked her in a gentle voice. "He's gone." He put a hand up, but somehow knew not to touch her. "Are you injured? Can I call the police for you?"

What would it matter? What would the police do about some guy she couldn't even identify beyond his halitosis?

The trembling persisted.

"No," she choked out. "I live close by here. I need to get home." She reached one hand behind her and grabbed her pants closed.

"Okay, I'll walk you." He scanned up and down the street. "You're trembling. You're probably in shock. Is there someone you can call to come be with you?"

She turned to face the man, trying to process what he said. "Um, yes."

"Okay, call someone, then get some juice. Do you have any juice in your house?"

She nodded.

"Okay, drink a big glass of juice and wrap yourself in a blanket. And get some rest. If, after the trembling stops, you feel you can talk to the police, call them and file a report."

She nodded again.

They arrived at her apartment building. A nice building in a bad area. Not the best combination for a single girl. Any girl. She lifted her key on her wrist strap, unlocked the door and turned toward her guardian angel.

"Thank you. You saved my life."

He gave her a small smile. "You're going to be fine." Then he stepped back and watched the door close as she walked into the building.

She heard the door automatically lock behind her. She pressed the elevator button and waited an eternity for it to arrive. She kept it together during her whole ride up to the fourth floor and her apartment. She locked the door behind her and went to the kitchen for juice. She thought of her guardian angel. Was he a doctor? After her juice, she stripped out of her clothes and climbed into the shower.

It got hot quickly, and that was just what she needed. A scalding hot shower to wash away the memory of her attack. But she couldn't stand any longer. She sank to the shower floor, crawled into a ball and wailed. She would have screamed if she didn't have neighbors on both sides of her. She was mugged, almost raped, and possibly killed tonight. Her life could have ended tonight.

After who knows how long, she dragged herself out of the shower and threw on a robe. She texted the PA, production assistant, and Gloria to tell them she could not be on the set in the morning. Then she turned off her phone and climbed into bed. Her sleep sucked. She tossed and turned and had nightmares all night.

In the morning, she hauled her body to the kitchen and made a cup of coffee. She would not cry yet; she needed to keep it together that morning. There was one call she'd need to make today. The one to her parents.

She turned on her cell phone and saw two texts. The PA was, of course, pissed at her. The second text was from Gloria wishing her well and telling her the director wasn't too bothered with the news since the day's filming didn't involve her. Lucky her.

She dialed her parents' place in upstate New York. God, how she missed them right now. Her eyes were blurry when her mom picked up the phone.

"Hello?"

"Hi, Mom." Her throat felt thick just hearing her mother's voice.

"Alex, what's wrong?"

"Oh God, Mom. I was walking home from the studio last night, and I was mugged." Tears streamed down her cheeks unbidden.

Her mother gasped. "Oh no. Are you alright?"

Her father picked up another phone and got on the line. "Alexandra, are you alright?"

"I'm fine. Just really shaken."

"Have you called the police?" her father asked.

"No, but I have nothing to tell them. I never saw his face."

"Oh, baby." Alex could hear her mother crying softly.

"Alexandra," her father started in a gentle tone, "would you *please* think about coming home now?"

She paused, considering her father's words. Did she really want to stay in this town anymore when she didn't feel safe?

"I'm coming home, Dad."

She heard her mother's sigh. "Oh, thank God. What can we do to help?"

"Nothing, Mom. I'll finish up filming in a few days, load everything in a moving van and fly home to New York."

"Alexandra, at least call the police and file a report. Describe whatever you do remember. That incident needs to be on record."

"Okay, Dad."

"Call us if you need anything, Sweetie. We'll see you soon," her mom said in a watery voice. The sound of her mother's anguish made her cry harder.

She kept it together long enough to say, "Mom, don't worry. I'm fine. I'll talk to you guys soon."

"We love you."

"I love you guys, too," and she hung up the phone. And gave herself permission for one good cry. At least she was going home.

Alex finished her coffee and croissant and called the non-emergency number of the LAPD. She was asked to come to the police station so that she could file a report. She dressed, threw on a bit of makeup to look presentable, and within forty minutes she was walking through the front door of the police station.

The receptionist picked up the phone and spoke to a detective. "Detective Beam will be with you in a moment," she informed her as she hung up the phone.

After a few short moments, an attractive thirty-something man walked up to her in the waiting area.

"Miss Marshall," he extended his hand. "I'm Detective Beam. Would you please follow me back to my desk?"

She rose and followed him through the double doors into the bustling station, passing several people working at desks. He turned back to her, "Can I get you anything to drink?"

"No, thank you."

He stopped at the end of a row of desks and motioned for her to sit at his desk. He took a seat behind the desk, opposite to her and situated the keyboard in front of him.

"I understand you were attacked last night and would like to file a report."

"Yes."

"I'll get some basic information from you first, then you can tell me what happened."

He kept his voice gentle and attentive the whole time he spoke to her. She saw an intensity in his eyes that told her he understood what she was going through. "Now, please tell me what happen. Take your time."

Again, that gentle voice. His voice reminded her of her guardian angel from the night before—full of compassion and understanding. She blinked rapidly. She needed to keep it together long enough to get through the story.

"It was just after midnight," she began and recounted all that she could. It was too fresh, too real.

She saw him reach for a box of tissues from a drawer and place them on the desk. Curious. Until she understood why—a tear fell from her cheek onto her hand resting on her lap.

She grabbed a tissue and wiped her cheeks and eyes and continued.

"Do you know who your guardian angel, as you put it, was? Did he give you his name?"

Alex shook her head. "No, and I didn't think to ask. I guess I was still so shaken. That probably would have been helpful, in case he saw my attacker, right?"

"Don't beat yourself up. It was dark out. Chances are slim he would have given us much information we could go on. The first thing I will do, Miss Marshall, is start a database search to see if your attack matches the description of other attacks in the area. That may help us gain leads." Then he pulled his business card out of the top drawer in his desk. "If you remember anything else, please don't hesitate to call me," and he gave her a smile that was both reassuring and sympathetic.

"Yes, of course," she managed to get out.

"And I have your number, so any progress I make, I'll give you a call."

Honestly, she thought, the chances of finding the bastard were slim to none.

He rose, so she did too. He presented his hand and she took it; he kept his eye contact and placed his other hand over hers. His hands felt warm and firm. "Take care, Miss Marshall."

He was kind, and Alex felt a prickling sensation on the backs of her eyes. "Thank you, Detective." And she stepped away from his desk and made her way to the front lobby.

Concentrate. Breathe. Do not cry.

That night she called Gloria. "Hey. How did it go today?" Alex asked.

"Long and boring. How are you? Are you sick? Do you think you will be able to make it back tomorrow?"

"I'll be there. I . . ." Suddenly her throat felt thick trying to articulate her words. "I was attacked last night on the way home."

Gloria gasped. "Oh shit. Are you alright?"

"Yes. Hell, I don't know. I was so scared. He had a knife and cut my pants and would have done more had someone not seen us and yelled."

"Oh God, Alex. Do you want me to come over?"

"No, the worst is over. I don't think I'll be going out at night for a while." *At least not in LA.*

"Did you tell the police?"

"Yes, I did that today." She took a deep breath. "I also called my parents. Gloria, I'm not staying. I mean, I'll finish this job, but then I'm moving back to New York."

"Oh wow. Really? I understand, but I'm gonna miss you."

"I gonna miss you too." She felt the tears threatening, so she blinked hard to fight them back.

"You'll be there tomorrow, so I'll see you in the morning."

"Yeah, see you in the morning." She disconnected the call.

Alex double-checked the locks and window blinds and shut off all but one light. She made her way into the bathroom and froze. The clothes she had on last night sat rumpled in a corner of the bathroom. How had she missed that this morning?

She would not cry. She would not cry.

She gathered the garments, went to the kitchen and shoved them—with some fury—down in the trash bag.

She kept her emotions in check, but she suddenly felt the urge for a shower. She hastily scrubbed every inch of her body, thankful the heat started to soothe her nerves. By the time she'd dried off, exhaustion finally settled in. She put on cotton undies and an oversized t-shirt and climbed into bed. Tomorrow was a new day. She had survived the attack, and she needed to remember that.

CHAPTER THREE

COLE HEARD HIS phone ring. Only one person would call him on a Saturday morning.

"Hey, sis."

"Hey. You ready to go shopping?" Cole could hear the enthusiasm in her voice.

"Not really."

She chuckled. "I'm at the spa. Meet me at Barney's in thirty minutes, okay?"

"Sure," he disconnected the line. Lauren had a plan to break away from the spa early to take him shopping. Shopping. Yeah, that's just what he wanted to be doing on a Saturday. No time was a good time for shopping. But Lauren had insisted he needed a better wardrobe if he was to work in an uptown, upscale spa. Not to mention gay guys didn't look like "shlumps", her words. He was a remodeler; he wasn't expected to wear a suit. Geez!

Whatever.

Three hours later, Cole sagged in a chair in the men's section of Saks for a few remaining items, according to Lauren. Placed on the floor beside him sat four shopping bags full of clothes and shoes. That didn't include the three suits that were being altered. Damn, that woman wore him out.

And just when he had a few moments to close his eyes, Lauren approached holding a pink and blue stripe tie. "I like this tie."

"You're kidding," he scowled.

"You're gay," she whispered.

Shit. He let his head drop back on the chair and closed his eyes trying desperately not to think about what else she picked out for him.

He heard Lauren give the sales girl her credit card to ring up the purchases then seconds later she flopped down next to him.

"Good day. I think we got most everything you'll need." She glanced down at the bags. "Five shirts, several pairs of pants, one blazer, three suits, six ties, and two pairs of shoes."

"Don't forget the bottle of cologne," he called out without opening an eye.

"You need to smell good, to fit in. Besides it smells good on you," she quipped.

He heard her take a deep breath. "I'll call Diane to come over and give you a trim tomorrow. Monday we'll go introduce you to everyone."

"Oh, joy and rapture," he grumbled.

True to her word, Sunday, at about eleven Lauren's friend, Diane, showed up at their place with a canvas bag over her shoulder.

"Hi, Di." She hugged her friend.

"Hey Lauren. How's it goin'? Where's my victim?"

Lauren smiled and turned to wave her hand toward the kitchen where Cole sat reading the news on his tablet.

"Hi Diane," Cole called from the kitchen. He closed the cover and pushed the tablet to the center of the table.

Diane strolled to the table, plopped her bag down and immediately reached for his hair.

Combing her fingers through, she said, "You got a good head of hair, Cole. I have wanted to get my hands on it for years."

Diane was a huge flirt. *It* could have been his hair or just about anything else of his.

"Yeah. Yeah. Just don't scalp me," he groaned.

Diane let out a laugh that sounded flirty, but slightly devious too. Lord, help him.

Thirty minutes later, Diane pulled off the cape around Cole's shoulders and announced, "Voila!"

Lauren looked up from the vegetables on the chopping board and said, "Wow, Di. That looks nice."

Nice. Did he get a nice haircut? He smoothed a hand down the back of his neck, feeling the shortness he hadn't felt since junior high. He stood and trudged to the bathroom to get a full look. Okay, it was short in the back but she didn't scalp him. No, it actually looked pretty good. Yeah. Not bad at all.

He returned to the kitchen. "It looks good, Diane. Thanks."

"It looks better than good, lover boy. It's fantastic, and women will love to get their hands on that head."

Cole bit back a chuckle at her innuendo. He leaned down to hug and thank her again. Then she completely surprised him by grabbing his face with her two hands and slamming a big, loud kiss on his lips.

Then she snatched her purse, gave Lauren a peck on the cheek saying, "Bye, love. Call me later so we can get together before you take off," and she was out the door.

He turned to look at Lauren, who was just smiling. He shook his head. "So you didn't tell her the full extent of the 'plan'?"

"No. I didn't see it as necessary. I think the fewer people that know, the better."

"Definitely."

He sat back down thinking about their unprecedented and stupendous plan. Lauren successfully turned him into a clean-cut, polished, high-class guy. At least from the looks of him. Now came his part—acting gay for four weeks. That might be hardest thing he'd ever had to do.

Colton Knight loved women. He loved the feel of a woman—her soft skin, her breath on his neck, the curve of her breast, tunneling deep inside her. He loved the taste of a woman, the smell. He'd never been in love, but that didn't matter. He could still appreciate a woman's laugh, her flirtatious glance, a smile that was just for him. Oh yeah. It was going be tough. He should probably ask Lauren for hazard pay.

***

Monday morning, Lauren and Cole strode off the elevator on the top floor toward the spa door. There was a small lobby before entering the spa itself, which covered the whole floor. Lauren unlocked the frosted glass door with L'Eclisse elegantly printed on it and proceeded to show him where the alarm was so he could disarm and rearm it every day and where the light switches were.

"Most days, I get in about twenty minutes before the girls. I've got Gretchen in charge of running the computer and teaching you the basics to log sales and appointments. Andrea will go over all the spa's offerings. The main goal this week, however, is introducing you to the clientele and easing you into place."

They walked back to the office and turned on Lauren's computer. Then, she gave him a quick tour of the enormous spa. There was a large room for pedicures and manicures. Smaller rooms for services like facials and massages and—apparently, a spa favorite—the steam room. Lastly, they went to the kitchen where Lauren started a pot of coffee and a pot of herbal tea, then turned on the stereo system. The door chimed which signaled the staff arrival.

Lauren looked up over at Cole. "You ready?"

"Ready as I'll ever be."

They strode to the front and greeted Andrea. "Andrea," Lauren announced, "this is my brother, Colton."

"Hello, Andrea. Good to meet you."

"Hi, Colton." She smiled up at him and shook his hand. "Lauren's told us about you coming to help out for a few weeks. So glad you'll be here fillin' in."

"I'm excited," he lied with a smile on his face.

Gretchen arrived just then and smiled as she noticed the group huddled around the reception counter.

"Gretchen," Lauren called, "this is my brother Colton. He'll be filling in for me while I'm away."

She offered her hand and said, "Great to meet you."

"You too." So far, the conversation didn't require much "acting" from his part, which was a relief.

"Why don't I show you the basics on the computer, Colton," Gretchen said as she walked behind the counter to drop her purse in a drawer.

"Sounds good. I know I've got big shoes to fill, but Lauren assures me that I'll be in good hands." He grinned.

After a few minutes of instruction on how to log in and open the necessary programs on the computer, another two women strolled in. Cole was introduced to Margie and Deanna, the massage therapist and aesthetician.

The phone rang and Gretchen answered cheerfully and pointed to the computer so Cole could watch as she booked an appointment. He focused his attention on the screen, but couldn't help overhear Margie whisper to Deanna how cute she thought he was and what a shame it was that he was gay. He bit back his grin. Gretchen finished the call, and then brought out a narrow three-ring binder.

"You can look up any of the processes in this book in case you forget what I've shown you."

"Okay."

"In about ten minutes, Mrs. Carmichael will arrive. She's been coming to the spa every Monday morning for years." She glanced down at the screen again and pointed, "It looks like she's getting Dysport and a mani-pedi."

"Dysport?"

"It's like Botox."

"Oh," he nodded. *Would a gay guy know that?*

"She will get her Dysport treatment first then relax in the chairs," Gretchen pointed to the large leather chairs across the spa, "and drink her herbal tea." Then she glanced at her watch. "If one of the girls doesn't show or is late, Andrea or I fill in. We cannot do things like Botox or fillers, but we can do most everything else—manicures, pedicures, massages, waxing. So hopefully Leigh will arrive soon."

Gretchen went back to teaching more operations on the front computer when a mid-sixties looking woman breezed in and slipped her sunglasses into her Prada bag. And right on cue, Lauren arrived from the back office to greet her.

"Mrs. Carmichael, how are you today?"

"Fine, Lauren. Thank you. And who do we have here?" she said giving a speculative once-over of Cole.

"Allow me to introduce my brother, Colton. Colton, this is Mrs. Carmichael, one of our most loyal clients. Colton will be filling in for me while I'm away on family business."

"Good to meet you, ma'am," and Cole held out his hand while giving one of his best smiles. Then he did just what he'd been dreading all week—he gave Mrs. Carmichael a dead-fish handshake. "And may I add, that bag is fabulous." He'd practiced saying that word and gave a subtle shake of the head at the same time.

Her eyes lit up at his demeanor and compliments.

"Why thank you, dear. I had my girl at Saks put it aside for me when it first arrived," she said looking down at her bag and smoothing a hand over it. "I do love it."

"Deanna is ready for you, Mrs. Carmichael, and I've made green tea with ginger today," she said as she escorted her client to a private room.

"Oh, perfect dear. Good for my arthritis."

Cole heard the door chime again and looked over to see a twenty-something woman with pigtail braids hustle in and bolt to the computer to sign in.

"Hi, guys. You must be Colton, Lauren's gay brother. Nice to see you. Sorry, I can't chat. I'm running late."

Obviously.

"That was Leigh. I guess I can introduce you to her later," Gretchen said.

Cole heard the scuttle of Leigh's feet on the carpet as she double-timed it to the break room. Moments later she skittered to the leather pedicure chairs to prepare for Mrs. Carmichael.

After a forty-minute break for lunch, Andrea provided a thorough education on the services the spa offered. By the end of the day, his head was swimming—Botox, Dysport, a slew of other injectables, fillers, permanent makeup, scrubs, cellulite treatments, waxing, and the ever-popular steam room with eucalyptus. It was amazing to him that women had time to work, have a social life or run a household with all the beauty treatments they underwent. Of course, the goal of looking good for the opposite sex goes back to before recorded history, and Cole, for one, was immensely thankful.

Lauren strolled to the front desk, propped her folded arms on the desk and asked, "How did it go?"

Cole tilted his head back to meet her gaze and let out an exaggerated exhale. "I survived."

Her lips curled up slightly, and the corners of her eyes crinkled. "I knew you would. How 'bout we get out of here?"

"I was hoping you'd say that." He stood and reached to turn off the monitor as the computer shutdown.

Lauren hit the lights and spoke as she armed the security alarm, "The girls are very good at keeping their areas clean throughout the day and in between customers. The professional cleaners come in at night, usually between ten and eleven. If something doesn't look right, their number is in the three-ring binder I showed you earlier in the office."

"Yes, I remember." Cole nodded.

"Any questions so far?" she asked as they waited for the elevator to arrive.

"Nope, I got almost everything answered today by Gretchen or Andrea. But I'm sure I'll think of something." As they walked onto the elevator, Cole wrapped a hand around her upper arm, "Are you nervous, Lauren?"

She scrunched her lips and shrugged her shoulders slightly.

"Don't be. Everything's going to be fine. You have everything so organized, and the girls are so well-trained that you have nothing to fear. We'll be good for four weeks."

She peered straight ahead for a while and exhaled. She looked up at him.

"You're right. The spa's in good hands. I'll just wrap up things in Paris and be back before you know it."

He heard her words and believed she had a certain amount of confidence in him and the girls, but that didn't lessen the pit in his stomach. He smiled and nodded, knowing he needed to pretend confidence when in fact he felt the exact opposite.

***

The week progressed without incident. Well, except for Suzanna Richardson. Lauren informed him it was always "Suzanna", never Suzie, Suzan or Suz. Although after meeting her, any one of those nicknames would have far suited her better. She was a pistol.

He remembered when *Suzanna* strolled into the spa—designer from head to toe—and her particular selections were more form fitting. Curves galore. Her eyes seemed to light up when she saw Cole standing at the counter. Lauren had made the introductions and despite Colton's act, Suzanna flirted and played with him shamelessly. Lauren finally got her to her way to her treatments.

An hour later, Suzanna reappeared wearing . . . towels. *Crap!* She sauntered to the counter with a little towel wrapped around her waist, barely hanging on, and another one draped around her neck barely covering her breasts. She had more skin showing than not. Suzanna clearly embraced the clothing optional aspect of the spa. Not that Cole took issue with it entirely. The woman had a shapely, well-treated body.

"Colton," she said as she came around the counter to give him a full view of her body. Her nearly naked body. Cole remained calm, in spite of a surge of energy that jolted his cock.

"I have some time today, so I'd like to see if Tara is available for a pedicure."

"Alright, let me see," he replied as he focused on the screen to check the schedule. "I'm sorry. She's expecting a client in a few minutes. I can certainly put you with someone else if you'd like." He plastered on a smile and turned back toward her awaiting a response.

"No," she sighed, "that's okay. I'll just sit in the steam room for a while."

He thought she would leave the area, but she quickly stopped and spun around to face him fully again.

"Colton, I know I've just met you, but I need a man's opinion, and I somehow feel that I can trust you to be honest with me."

Without any forewarning, she flung the towel from off her shoulders, leaving her completely topless in front of him.

She took a step closer to him. "I've recently had my boobs redone. Do you think they're too big?"

Oh, fuck.

"Be honest." She turned her chest presenting him with a profile view from the right, then the left. "What do you think?"

What could he say? For her frame, the Double-D cups might be a bit much? *Nah.* He could ask to see how they felt in his hands, but for one, she would say yes, and two, he needed to quit thinking like a guy. *Dammit!*

He took a deep breath. "I think they're simply fantastic. I don't know who your doctor is, but I recommend you not let too many people know because they'll go to him out of jealousy of those amazing mammaries." Then he placed his hands on his hips and shifted his weight to his right side giving a matter-of-fact look.

The smile that came across her face was genuine. Her back straightened and she replied, "Thank you, Colton. You're a doll." And finally she left. He'd wiped the beads of sweat from his brow.

He remembered just barely getting through that day with his sanity intact. It might be best to check when she was due to return to the spa, so he could hide in the back office.

CHAPTER FOUR

THREE IN THE afternoon, Alex's plane landed at La Guardia airport, leaving Los Angeles behind. She was sad to leave her friends, but she needed a fresh start. The attack had shaken her to the core. Being with family is where she needed to be, and like her parents had said, there are plenty of acting jobs in New York.

She would likely search out an acting coach to help her adjust to stage acting versus film, but that didn't worry her in the least. She was good—not great—but good enough to hold her own.

First priority was housing and a job waitressing. That would pay the bills and give her the flexibility to go on calls and auditions as needed. She'd find an agent who, no doubt, would send her on small gigs until he or she felt comfortable enough to send her on bigger jobs. Alex was fine with that. She could pay her dues and work her way up. It might take a few years, but this is what she loved. Acting was all she ever wanted to do.

Well, except for that brief time she thought she'd be a singer, then a director, and then a fashion model. Yet every time, she came back to acting. She smiled slightly as she yanked her carry-on from the compartment overhead.

She exited and moved with the crowd to baggage claim. One or both of her parents would be waiting for her there. She smiled again at the thought of seeing them again. Living in LA, she didn't get back as often as she'd like to see her parents or her brother. In fact, it had been several months since she'd seen them last.

"Alexandra!" She heard her name and glanced to her right to spy her parents, John and Janine, smiling at her, waiting.

"Hi, Mom." She placed her bag and purse down and hugged her mother. Then reached up to hug her six-foot beefy father. "Hi, Dad."

"Hi, pumpkin. How are you? How was your flight?" It was funny, Alex thought, how everyone always seemed to ask that question.

"I'm good, and the flight was good. How are you guys?"

They chatted as they made their way closer to the baggage carousel and waited for her suitcases to appear.

"You're letting your hair grow," her mom noticed.

"Yeah. I like how easy it is to whip up in a ponytail when I need."

"Aidan will be up for dinner tomorrow night. When does the rest of your stuff arrive?" her mom asked.

"Thursday. So that gives me a week to find a place in the city to live. I have the number of the moving van driver. I'm supposed to call him with an exact address. If I can't find something, I guess everything will have to come to Kingston, which will cost me extra."

"Don't worry about that, Alex. You'll find something. Will you stay with Aidan while you look?" Her dad grunted as he retrieved her first heavy suitcase.

"Yeah. I asked him if I could stay for the week until I got my own place and a job. Of course, he said I could take as long as I wanted, but I don't particularly want to sleep on Aidan's sofa." She smiled and rolled her eyes.

They loaded her luggage into the family car parked out front and started the two-hour drive to Kingston. Along the way, Alex got the full update of her extended family, the farm, the town, all of it. In some respects, it was like she never missed a beat. Like she hadn't been gone for more than five years.

Without prying heavily, her parents asked about her case in LA, and if the police found anything. The detective on the case had called her once, saying that just because she might not have heard from him didn't mean the case was dead. He was very sweet. She told him she'd be moving to New York and, if Alex wasn't mistaken, he sounded a little disappointed.

"No, Mom, nothing."

"Well, we're just glad you're home, sweetie." Alex knew that statement held multiple meanings.

"Me too." She sank deeper into the backseat, took a deep breath and let the peace and security envelope her. She was home. She was alive, and she was home.

Aidan arrived the next evening an hour before dinner. He called out from the front door, "Alex!"

"What? You don't have to yell. I can hear you."

He walked into the kitchen where she stood cutting up potatoes for dinner. Coming up beside her, he swiftly wrapped his arms around her and lifted her off the ground.

"Ah," she shrieked. "Put me down, you brute!"

"Get a job, you slacker." He released her. She dropped her knife on the cutting board and turned to give him a proper hug.

She and Aidan were reasonably close, now that they were adults. Growing up, they would argue and tease each other mercilessly. Now the teasing meant nothing except to show affection and admiration for one another.

"I'm tryin'. You gonna let me bunk with you for a while so I can find something?"

"Bunk as long as you want, sis. I missed you." He released her and mussed the top of her head with his hand.

She narrowed her eyes at him and smoothed her hair. "I know. What's not to miss?" She shrugged a shoulder and smiled sweetly.

"So where's Mom?" he asked.

"Mom's in the garden. She's making a pot roast for dinner." Her father strode into the kitchen and placed his truck keys on the desk.

"Excellent. I didn't eat lunch so I can wholly partake in the goodness." Aidan smiled full-on showing his pearly whites, then walked out the screen door to the garden in the back to find his mother.

The next day, after helping their parents around the farm for a bit, their dad drove them to the train station. Janine packed a lunch for them. Once a mom, always a mom. Alex smiled, hoping that would never change.

On the train ride to Penn Station, Aidan talked about his job working as a corporate trainer. His company, a big New York bank, treated him well. He started working for them right after college, survived severe layoffs in 2008, and would soon get another promotion. That excited him because it meant more responsibility and the opportunity to travel.

He asked Alex about her acting jobs and delicately broached the subject of the attack. She relished that big-brother protectiveness when he spoke about her staying at his place for a while. She was quite certain he wanted to keep an eye on her and make sure she was safe.

"How does steak sound for dinner?" he called out from the kitchen.

"Great."

"You get settled. Make yourself at home. I have work to do in the office."

"Okay, thanks."

Aidan had a nice apartment. His salary allowed him to have a two-bedroom place so the second bedroom could be used as an office. Unfortunately, there was only one bed—his. He graciously let her take it, since he had no issues sleeping on the sofa. She didn't argue with him over it. She knew all of it would only be temporary. Starting tomorrow she would look for a place to live and possibly a job. It would be tricky finding a place without proof of income, but she'd figure something out.

***

After some discussion with Aidan the day before, Alex came up with a plan for her job search and, more importantly, her apartment search.

He recommended she start in the East Village. The apartments were smaller with fewer amenities, but they were cheaper too. So Sunday she stepped out of Aidan's apartment building, street map in hand.

She scoped out a few bars and restaurants along the way, making a note to hit them later when they were open. She walked into her first apartment building. The place had a subtle smell of . . . fish. The man at the front desk looked up from his smartphone. The nose ring was distracting but she cast her focus to his eyes.

"Hello. I'm looking for a one-bedroom place. Do you have anything available?"

"Yeah." He stood slowly, walked to the cabinet beside the desk and retrieved a key. "Follow me. It's on the fourth floor. It's unfurnished, you know."

"That's fine." Unless it was immaculate or had an amazing view, she probably wasn't going to take it.

He opened the door and the fish smell was gone. It had been replaced by dog, wet dog. She resisted the urge to gag.

"How long has this apartment been vacant?" she asked.

"About a month."

Weird. She stepped inside to glance around. "Do you allow pets?"

"No way."

He gave her the price, relocked the door and they made their way back to the front desk.

"I'll think about it and get back to you. Thanks."

"Uh-huh," and dropped his head down to stare at his phone.

Alex walked outside and inhaled the fresh air.

She walked up and down the streets, checking off the apartments one at a time. She was striking out. *Damn!*

Some were too cramped or had paper-thin walls. One showed promise, but the next-door neighbor peered his hairy body out to look at her and the leasing rep, and he looked positively spooky. Even the rep tensed.

Alex decided to head back to Soho and hit a few bars to see if they had any openings.

She arrived at the first place, a bar and grill with a honky-tonk feel. The manager was friendly but said he didn't have any openings. He took her number anyway, in case something opened up, he said.

The next place seemed more upscale. It was a bar that hosted musical acts most nights. The hostess took her name and said the manager, also the owner, would call her the next day. Evidently he was off on Sundays, but the hostess expected there might be a need since one of their waitresses would be heading back to college in the fall. Alex relished the first tiny glimmer of hope all day.

She trudged into a coffee shop for a little pick-me-up. She settled on a turkey sandwich and a raspberry iced tea. She must have looked like she was withering away because a cute guy let her cut in front of him to order. His looks reminded her of some famous actor, but she couldn't think of the name right then. Lack of nutrition.

"Thanks," she smiled at him.

She hit a few more restaurants and bars on the way back to Aidan's. Now it was just a waiting game. The wait for the calls to come in asking for an interview.

Aidan strolled into the apartment, after coming from his girlfriend's apartment shortly before six. Alex had prepared a chicken dish and a salad for dinner, more than enough for two.

"Hi Alex," he said sauntering into the kitchen. "How'd it go today?"

"Um, so-so. Found a few places I could work, now it's just a matter of giving it time. But the apartment hunting was brutal."

He reached into the fridge for a beer and faced her, "Don't worry about it. Stay here as long as you need."

"Thanks, Aidan. I may have to take you up on that, but regardless, I'll hit it again tomorrow."

He took a swig of his beer when his cell phone rang.

"Hello?"

"Hey, Ace. I need your help."

"Sure, man."

Cole couldn't believe what he was about to ask. "Do you have any cufflinks?"

He heard Ace mumble something to someone else about being right back. "Yeah, I've got some you can borrow. When did you want them?"

"I was hoping to swing by tonight."

"That's fine. I think I mentioned my sister moved back to New York, and she's staying with me. She's here now, so what do you want me to tell her?"

"I think I should play it safe and keep everything a secret. I've got three weeks left. Then I can let her know the truth."

"Okay. See you in a few?"

"Yeah. Thanks," He hung up the phone.

Cole vaguely remembered Alex. She had short, straight brown hair and always seemed, giddy. She was three years younger than Aidan, so it wasn't like they all hung out together.

As boys they were into sports and playing things like cops and robbers. Girls, like Alex played with dolls and seemed to always be giggling. Something that drove him crazy, and that might be another reason why he barely remembered her. Why he'd avoided her.

After a short ten minutes, he rang the bell at Ace's place. "C'mon in," he said.

Cole meandered in and watched Ace pick up a box and hand it to him.

"Alex, wanna come here?"

She walked out of the kitchen toward the two men.

"Do you remember Cole?"

Cole nearly fell over reaching to shake her hand. Alex looked nothing like what he remembered. She had long brown hair with a little wave in it and subtle sunny highlights that framed her face and eyes. And her eyes, her beautiful brown eyes, spellbinding.

She was taller now, maybe five-eight; and her body, perfect curves in just the right places. His body stirred. Alex had turned into an attractive woman.

If only I didn't have to act gay.

"Good to see you again," he said as he shook her delicate, warm hand. He pulled back and scratched the side of his stubbled face.

"Good to see you again too. We're getting ready to eat. Care to join us?"

His eyes darted quickly to Aidan then back to her. "Oh, thanks but I should be getting back." His heart jackhammered at the thought of staying and interacting with Alex as a *gay* man. He needed to calm the hell down.

"No, you should stay. We have plenty." She motioned with her arm toward the kitchen behind her. "We just opened a bottle of white wine, would you like a glass?"

"Uh, sure." He glanced at his friend who just shrugged at him.

Alex poured a glass of wine and handed it to him. She smiled brightly.

This might be a good time to bring out Colton. He sipped with his pinky slightly raised.

"This tastes fabulous. Thank you. Well, since I appear to be staying, I'll just go wash up before dinner."

Alex nodded and turned back to the kitchen to pull a big casserole dish out of the oven.

Cole passed by Aidan and narrowed his eyes. Ace bit back a grin and shrugged his shoulders. Again.

Aidan damn well knew this was going to be a challenge for him.

After Cole left the room, Alex moved two steps over to Aidan. "Is it my imagination or is Cole . . . gay?" she whispered.

"It's not your imagination."

"Damn." Alex had practically swooned when Cole walked in. His gorgeous green eyes captivated her. Then she glimpsed at his sculptured lips and strong jawline, his rock-hard chest on his toned, muscular body. His tall frame topped off with yummy dark blonde hair. She could so easily grab his face and tongue-kiss him so deep he'd cry Uncle. *If only he weren't gay.*

Dinner went better than expected. Everyone ate heartily. The guys told stories from when they grew up in Kingston. Funny stories Alex hadn't heard before.

The camaraderie between Cole and her brother was the best. An outsider might think they were brothers.

They all laughed, and the air at the table was easy. Despite the regret about Cole being gay, Alex enjoyed her evening.

The tiny box resting beside Cole caught her eye. "What's in the box?"

"Oh, I've got this new shirt with French cuffs, but can't seem to find my cufflinks. Aidan was gracious enough to lend me his," he said with a smile. "It'll look great with just a blazer and no tie, I think."

Alex felt distracted by Cole, and she couldn't figure out why. Her cell phone rang, interrupting her thoughts.

"Excuse me," she muttered and jumped up from the table. *Gloria?* "Hello?"

"Alex, it's Gloria. You are not gonna believe what I'm holding in my hand?"

"Hey. What is it?"

"It's your ring," she almost squealed in Alex's ear.

"Are you kidding me?" Alex froze. Her heart rate skyrocketed, and her mouth went dry.

"No. I'd recognize it anywhere. It was in a pawnshop. I dashed in on a whim last night when Barry and I went out for dinner." She sounded as excited as Alex felt. "So I need an address to mail it to you."

Alex felt overcome with emotion. She sank to the sofa. Tears streamed down her face. She never thought she'd see that ring again. She loved it because it was beautiful, but also because her parents had given it to her.

"Alex?"

"Yeah, I'm here. Gloria, I can't thank you enough," she sobbed.

"Hey. Hey. Sweetie, it's alright. No need to cry."

She looked up and caught a sight of Aidan and Cole watching her with concern written on their faces.

"I'm okay," she said for their benefit and Gloria's. She gave her brother's address and asked how much Gloria spent so she could send her money.

"No, sweetie. No money. But when you make it big, don't forget all your friends out here in LA."

"You got it, chica! Thank you so much." And wrapping it up, she disconnected the line and set the phone back in her purse.

"Alex, what's wrong?" Aidan asked, a wrinkle evident in his forehead.

She blinked a few times and wiped her cheeks. "My friend, Gloria, found my ring in a pawnshop in LA."

"No way. That's awesome."

Cole stared at Aidan and then Alex, a blank look on his face.

Alex returned to the table and bit the inside of her cheek. She looked up at Cole. "I was attacked in LA. The guy took my purse and my ring. It was a ring my parents gave me after graduation from college. So, that was my friend and she said she found it in a pawnshop." The tears threatened to spill from her eyes again.

"That's incredible," Aidan said as he reached and cupped his warm hand over hers.

She smiled, and he smiled back at her. When she glanced over at Cole, he gave her a penetrating stare, one that she couldn't quite read.

"I'm glad you're alright," he said in a low voice.

The intensity and sincerity in his eyes drove straight to her being. "Yeah, I'm alright."

There was something in Cole's gaze that touched Alex. Maybe it was because he was more connected to his feminine side, she thought. She pushed her thoughts of Cole aside and focused herself back to the present.

"I'm just glad Gloria found my ring. That is the icing on the top of my day."

"Here. Here. Way to go, sis," Aidan called out as he raised a glass toward her. Cole joined in.

Alex took a deep breath and leaned forward with a straight back. "I'll drink to that," she took a sip of wine then rose to clear the dishes. "How about a little coffee, guys?"

"Yeah, sounds good."

"Sure."

As Alex strode to the kitchen, Aidan's cell phone rang. "Sorry guys. I'll be back in a minute."

Alex returned to the table to sit with Cole.

"The chicken dish was delicious. Thanks, Alex."

She smiled. "You're welcome. Glad you could join us."

He nodded. "Do you mind if I ask what happened in LA?"

"With the attack?" Alex replied.

"Yes."

She licked her lips. "No, I don't mind. I was leaving the studio late one night and as I walked home a guy jumped out and attacked me. He pushed me face-first against the brick wall, flashed a knife, he demanded my jewelry and purse."

She took a calming breath. "I had pepper spray on my keychain, but it fell out of my hand. Anyway, I handed him everything, but then . . . then he didn't leave. He cut the back of my pants as if to rape me." Alex heard a sharp intake of air. "I was lucky because right then a guy walked by on the main road and saw us. He yelled, and my attacker ran in the opposite direction."

"Alex, I am so sorry to hear that." She looked up and saw the sincerity in Cole's eyes. "Were the police able to find him?"

"No," she shrugged. "I didn't get a good look at him because of the way he had me pushed . . ." She stopped suddenly when the best idea popped into her head.

"What is it?"

Alex jumped up and ran to her purse to yank out her phone.

"What's going on?" Aidan asked as he strolled back to the table.

Alex looked up at the guys, her eyes aglow. "I didn't see my attacker, but what if there is a chance that he's on the video at the pawnshop?"

"Oh, yeah," Aidan chimed.

She quickly shot a text to Gloria. "I can get the address of the pawnshop and call the detective. Chances are my assailant is on their videotape. They might just get this guy," the tone of her voice rising with excitement.

"That would be awesome."

"Good luck, Alex," Cole added.

"Thanks." She smiled, feeling hopeful about the case for the first time since that horrific day.

CHAPTER FIVE

COLE UNLOCKED the spa door the next morning. He knew the routine for opening pretty well now. He went through the motions of setting up the coffeemaker while his thoughts wandered to Alex.

She had turned into a fine looking woman, no doubt about it. And a good cook, too. His lips curled slightly. But when she told the story of her attack in LA, it was all he could do to keep a poker face. His stomach roiled. He wanted to kill the guy who attacked her, and he didn't have thoughts like that often. He took some comfort in the fact that she was currently staying with Ace, but that wasn't going to last. He made a mental note to talk to Ace about that later.

Andrea, Gretchen, and the other girls started arriving. They briefly went over the appointments scheduled for the day before readying their stations.

A few minutes after one, Mrs. McMillan arrived for a massage and waxing. Cole knew from the prior week that she was a chatty woman.

"I am so sorry I am late. The installers came by my home this morning to hang my new living room drapes. You would not even believe what they did," she huffed. "They tried hanging them right above the window. I have twelve-foot ceilings! Are they looney?" Her voice rose an octave. "Everyone knows the way to make drapes look spectacular is to hang them all the way up the wall, with just *a little* puddling."

Cole processed what she explained, trying not to reveal his confusion. "No worries, Mrs. McMillan. Sounds like you were fortunate to be there to catch them before it turned positively disastrous," Cole said with an exaggerated hand gesture.

"You know Colton, you're right." She smiled at him and nodded firmly. "Crisis averted."

"Well, if you're ready," he walked out from behind the reception desk, "why don't we get you started? Can I get you a cup of herbal tea or a glass of chilled water?"

After getting Mrs. McMillan settled, Cole retreated to the back office to email Lauren. He wanted to keep Lauren up to date on things at the spa, and get an update on Aunt Rosie's estate. Since there was a six-hour difference, there was a possibility that she might be at her computer and they could possibly instant message.

Message sent, he waited. He worked on the computer while he waited. Lauren had shown him how to check product stock and where to reorder as needed. After thirty minutes, he figured she was tied up and went back on the floor.

***

Monday, Alex decided to take a break from apartment hunting to grab some lunch at a nearby deli in The Village. So far, the day brought mixed results. One place looked like it could be a winner, but the manager had someone else interested and said he would have an answer for her by tomorrow. Several places, which appeared clean and neat, wouldn't have openings until the end of the month. And as to be expected, a few were out of her price range.

The line for the deli went out the door, but it moved quickly. As she got closer to the counter to order, she glanced around in search of an open table. Scanning the room, she suddenly caught sight of the guy she ran into at the coffeehouse the day before.

He smiled and left his table to approach her. "Hey, small world. I'm Preston Murray," and he held out his hand.

"Hi. Alex Marshall."

"Care to join me for lunch?" he asked as he motioned to a little table in front of the window.

"Sure, I'd like that." A shy smile came across her lips.

Holy cow. What a surprise to run into this guy again in a city of millions! He was pretty good looking, too. He had a great smile, and Alex couldn't help notice an adorable chin cleft. It looked like he kept fit, which was a big plus for Alex. She wished he was a bit taller considering she was five-eight, but it was not like they were planning to get married tomorrow.

After a relaxed lunch, Preston asked for her number, and she gave it to him. They walked out together; he went left, and she went right. She couldn't help herself and glanced back and caught him looking and smiling at her. *Funny*. She gave him a little wave.

Her cell phone chimed, pulling her out of her thoughts. She had a voicemail. Weird, since she hadn't heard her phone ring in the deli. She stopped in front of a store and checked her messages. The manager of the bar she popped into yesterday left a message asking her to stop by and talk with him later today. Wouldn't it be great if he had something open now, she thought.

She powered through a few more apartment buildings, but nothing felt right. When did she become so picky? She needed to finish for today. Her feet were beginning to hurt and so did her back. She decided to make her way to the bar in Soho.

A man who appeared to be the manager sat at the bar writing on a clipboard. Alex approached him.

"Hello. I'm Alex Marshall. Are you the manager?"

He looked up from his work. He was a big man with a big smile and apples on his cheeks.

"You got him," he stuck out his hand. "Name's Ralph Smith. Have a seat, Alex." He had a big voice to match his frame. Loud and deep. She imagined he could be intimidating if he wanted.

She sidled up on the barstool beside him.

"So tell me a little about yourself."

Ah, the quintessential on-the-spot interview question. She'd a few of these in her lifetime. Managers or agents like to let you think it was an informal "chat" when indeed they were sizing you up. Alex launched into a brief history of college, acting, and the two waiting jobs she had in LA. She left off why she was back except to say her family lived in New York.

"Only two jobs while in LA. That's sorta unheard of."

"I liked where I worked, and I guess they liked me, so I didn't see the need to jump around. I can give you my previous manager's names so you can get references."

"Yeah, that would be good. Here's what's goin' on. My business has been growing steadily. I have a musical act on that stage almost every night. I got a gal who works part time and all she does is find, book and promote the acts for the bar. And damn, if she's not doing a hell of a job. So I'm looking for an experienced waitress, a . . . server to work nights. You'll probably be going to acting calls and such, right?"

"Yes."

"I figured as much. Got a few other actors working here too. I'll be as flexible as I can. Most of the time, you guys seem to juggle your own schedules and let me know when you wanna work." He grinned and shook his head. "Anyway," he slipped an application off his clipboard and pushed it toward her, "if you could fill this out, I'll check references. When can you start?"

She thought about an apartment-full of furniture coming Thursday that would need a home *somewhere*. "Friday."

"Great. Here's a pen. Fill this out and leave it here. I'll call you probably tomorrow to set things up." And he stood, his belly almost bumping into Alex.

"Great, thanks, Mr. Smith."

"Oh, call me Ralph. I'll talk to you tomorrow, Alex." With that he plodded to his office in the back.

Alex whipped out an index card with all the contact information she'd need for the application. She hadn't met the staff here, but it certainly seemed like a good place to work. Once completed, she left the sheet on the bar, hopped off the barstool and made her way to the front door.

She stepped out in the ninety-degree weather again. The manager all but offered her the job. She had a good feeling about this because there wouldn't be a problem with her references. She went back to Aidan's place, winding through pedestrians on the sidewalk. People probably thought she was crazy with a grin on her face. She bit her bottom lip. What a good day. Things were starting to fall into place.

Alex dragged her tired ass into Aidan's apartment and collapsed on the sofa. She didn't know what time it was when she heard her phone ring. Aidan had an overnight business trip and told her he would check in with her that evening.

"Hey."

"Hey, yourself. How'd it go today?"

"Slow. Pretty much struck out on the apartment hunting. I'll hit the pavement again tomorrow. I gotta believe that something will pop. Oh, but I do have good news. I got a call from a manager of a bar, so I stopped in to meet him. He interviewed me on the spot. It looks like I'll get an official offer soon."

"Great. When will you hear something?"

"Tomorrow or the next day and we didn't talk about the pay. How is it going in Chicago?"

"Good. No complaints. I expect to be home around six tomorrow. Oh, I gotta go. Jade's calling."

"Who's Jade?"

"My girlfriend." His voice dropped to a soft tone at the mention of her name.

"Ooh," she gave him a sassy taunt.

"Talk to you later," he disconnected the line.

She immediately texted him.

When do I get to meet said girlfriend?

After thirty minutes, he texted her back.

I'll invite her over this week. Maybe Thursday or Friday.

Sounds good, she replied.

Alex peeled herself off the sofa and went to the fridge to find something for dinner. The mound of casserole from the previous night sat front and center. She grinned. Lucky her. She heated a serving in the microwave, and as she set her plate on the table, the doorbell rang. She peeked through the peephole to see Cole standing, waiting, in a dark jacket and tan pants, looking very professional.

"Hi," she opened the door.

"Hi," he smiled. "I was on my way home from work and thought I'd drop by and see how it was going."

"Oh, c'mon in," she stepped back to give him room. "I'm doing fine."

As he strolled in, he caught sight of her dinner plate at the table. "Hey, I just wanted to drop by and check on you. I didn't mean to bother you during dinner."

"No. No bother. Have you eaten? If you don't mind leftovers, I'll heat some of last night's dish."

"That'd be great. Thanks." The corner of his mouth curved.

"This actually works out because I wanted to open a bottle of wine, but not for only myself," she grinned. As she loaded up a plate for Cole, she asked, "Why don't you open the chardonnay in the fridge?"

Alex had planned on eating, soaking in the tub and heading to bed early after some crap TV. Now she had a dinner companion, a handsome one at that.

As they ate, they chatted about her day and her lack of success in finding an apartment, and her on-the-spot interview with a bar manager. Then she asked about his work at the spa and filling in for Lauren.

"Today was my first official day on my own because Lauren just left Saturday. But so far so good."

"When I land a job, I'll have to come check it out."

"Girl, just let me know when. Your service will be on-the-house."

Her eyes widened. "Really?"

"Sure. You're Ace's sister. You're like family."

"Thanks, Cole. So any interesting stories to share yet? Any famous stars you got to meet?"

He nodded and grinned. "Just Friday I had a client flash my her boob job asking for my opinion."

Alex slapped her hand on her thigh, leaned forward, and chuckled. "No way."

"Yes way. I guess she felt comfortable. I don't know."

She leaned back in her chair. "Well, sure. She probably figured since you're gay you would make a good impartial judge."

"Oh yeah," he strung out the word. "I hadn't thought of that."

She chuckled at him, and he smiled.

Cole helped her clean up, and then she walked him to the door.

"Here," he pulled a card out of his jacket pocket and handed it to her. "This is my cell number. Call if you need anything, okay?"

She took the card and keeping his gaze, she nodded. "Okay. I will. Thanks."

Cole had a way of looking at her deep into her eyes, like he could see her soul. She saw caring and gentle eyes that were nearly impossible to read.

He smiled and pivoted, heading down the hall to the elevator. She watched him. A ridiculous hesitation kept her rooted at the doorway. He glanced her way while waiting for the elevator doors to open and smiled. She gave him a little wave as he stepped inside and out of sight.

She proceeded to the bathroom for a nice soak in the tub. Her muscles ached everywhere, and her feet were swollen and sore. As heat penetrated her muscles, she thought about dinner with Cole. What a thoughtful guy to check in on her. He probably felt compelled to check in on her since learning about her attack in LA. Regardless, she appreciated the care and attention. The corners of her lips curved. He would probably make a good bestie.

Then thoughts of her unproductive and frustrating day popped unwelcome in her head. Tomorrow she'd go after it again. If she didn't find something, she'd have to look outside of East Village, and God knew she couldn't afford that. She already going out on a limb for some place half the size of what she had in LA. She might need to consider getting a roommate. Admittedly, she felt the pressure bearing down on her.

Tomorrow. She'd think about it all tomorrow.

CHAPTER SIX

BEFORE HEADING to the spa on Tuesday, Cole needed to stop in on a kitchen remodel that was wrapping up. On his way, he thought about dinner the previous night with Alex.

Conversation with her was easy. She seemed smart and more than once she made him laugh with her wit. He vacillated over whether to stop by, but he was certainly glad he did.

Arriving at the job site, the homeowner greeted him at the door. "Wow! Cole, don't you look nice."

Shit. He'd gotten so used to wearing suits that he'd forgotten what he had on.

"Thanks, Mrs. Siegler. Got something to do after this, and I'm trying to look my best." Which was definitely the truth. "So how's everything shaping up? Why don't we go through the punch-list and see what we have left outstanding?"

Surveying the kitchen, he smiled to himself. His crew had done an exceptional job, as usual. The client glowed about everything, which made the workload he was now juggling worth it. There were a few lingering issues, things that required scheduling the right person to complete the task. Cole took some notes, then left to make his way to the spa.

Andrea had opened, and several employees and clients were already milling about when he arrived.

"Hey, Colton. Lauren called. She said to call her on her cell when you get in."

"Thanks, Andrea." He sauntered to the back office to make his call.

"Hello?"

"Hey sis, how's it going in Paris?"

"Hey, Cole. It's great here. I love this city." He could hear the enthusiasm in her voice, and that was another reason this whole act was worth it.

"I'm glad to hear it."

"Basically, I don't have much to report. I've met with the lawyer and the financial people. There will be more meetings, no doubt, but transferring assets to the US shouldn't be a huge deal. I took a tour of her house or should I say, mansion."

"No way."

"Way. Aunt Rosie had apparently invested wisely and was able to buy a huge house. So now I need to go through her things and sort everything in order to get the house ready to sell. Plus, I will need to host a memorial service for her."

"How are you supposed to do that?"

"Well, the lawyer is going to help me. Apparently they were friends. Maybe even more than friends, if you know what I mean."

Cole practically heard her smile. "Yes, I know what you mean."

"Anyway, that's pretty much all I have. I'm trying to adjust to the longer days here. It's strange seeing the sun set at ten o'clock." She chuckled.

Despite being alone, Lauren sounded good, and that's all Cole needed to know.

"Well, it's almost dinnertime for you, right? Why don't you go order a hamburger? I heard they put a fried egg on it."

She laughed again. "It's true. So how is everything at the spa?"

"Very good. Nothing to report. 'Course, it's only been one whole day without you."

"Oh, that's right. Well, I'll let you go. Mrs. Prestavich will likely be in this week. Remember she's going through a divorce, so treat her with kid gloves."

"I haven't forgotten. You take care of everything in Paris and get home soon."

"I will. Love you."

"Love you back." He hung up the phone. Unless it was his imagination, she sounded upbeat. That meant everything to him.

***

Alex awoke with renewed determination. It was Tuesday. She knew finding a decent place might not be easy, but there was something out there for her. There had to be, she thought.

She followed her map up a street in a part of the neighborhood she hadn't covered yesterday. From the looks of it, it was a quieter street, and the homes appeared older.

Eighteen-twelve, eighteen-fourteen, eighteen-sixteen . . . she had another block or so to go.

She heard a loud pop and jumped. She looked behind her left shoulder and noticed an older man fussing with his doormat.

He looked up at her wide eyes. "Oh, sorry, Miss. Didn't mean to startle you."

"Oh, it's fine," she murmured as she heard the blood pumping in her ears.

Beyond him, a movement caught her eye. Someone placed a sign in the first floor window of the house next door. Lovely building, but she couldn't quite make out the sign while the man continued to shake out his rug.

Alex turned and made her way up the street. "Have a nice day," the old man called.

"You too," she smiled in reply.

Eighteen-twenty, twenty-two . . . the weather felt pleasant; a perfect temperature to be outside. Despite herself, Alex felt an elusive panicky feeling come over her. She turned around and saw no one following her. In fact, the street was mostly bare. People were obviously at work.

An inexplicable fear washed over her. Her jaw clenched.

Something doesn't feel right about this situation, she said to herself. She froze in her tracks, looking, looking. Was someone watching her? She licked her lips and tried to calm her racing heart. She moved up against the wall, her back flat to it. It was broad daylight. No one would try anything now, right?

The older man from earlier called to her from his doorstep, "Miss, are you alright?"

Answer him.

The anxiety felt too great, too paralyzing. She merely stared at him and nodded twice. His eyebrows knit together, and his head tipped slightly.

"Are you sure? Do you want to sit down?" He propped his broom against the brick wall.

"Marguerite," he called out to his neighbor, "you might wanna come out here."

After a few beats, an older woman stepped out from the building next to his. "What is it, Hank?"

He nodded his chin up the street toward her and said, "She stopped suddenly, looking dazed. I think she's sick, or she's got dementia."

She turned her head and grimaced at him. "Young people don't get dementia, Hank," she scolded him.

"Sweetie, are you alright? Are you sick?" The older lady slowly paced her way to Alex. "Can I get you something to drink?"

Speak, Alex. "I think I'm having an anxiety attack," she managed to get out.

"Alright, so the best thing is to calm yourself first with some deep breaths." Her calm, confident voice quickly settled Alex's nerves. "Like this." The woman visibly inhaled, letting her whole torso move, and then exhaled audibly. "Now you give it a try."

Alex did as she was told.

"Good, now a little deeper."

Alex did it again. By that time, the older man had approached them and stood watch.

"How ya' doin'?" he asked like only New Yorkers could.

"I'm feeling better." And she was, she realized.

"Care to come back to my place for some lemonade?"

Alex's mom would make lemonade a lot during the summer. She said it would thin the blood and make you feel cooler. Who knows, but Alex knew it would be delicious and refreshing.

"Yes, that would be great. Thank you," she looked down at the woman.

She pushed off the wall, and the woman stepped back. "My name's Marguerite and this here's Hank."

"My name's Alexandra. Alex."

"Well, good to meet you, Alex," and he three walked back to her building. Alex stopped in her tracks, steps from the threshold, when the sign in Marguerite's front window struck Alex like a lightning bolt. *ROOM FOR RENT,* it read.

Marguerite paused and swirled around when she realized Alex wasn't behind them.

"Alex?"

"You have a room for rent, Marguerite?"

"Yes, I do. Just had it freshly painted after the last boarder left. Bought himself a house in Jersey." She scrunched up her nose at Alex, "You lookin' for a room?"

Fixing her eyes on the couple that might be her two new best friends, she said, "Yes," she smiled feeling the hope blossoming inside her. "Yes, I am."

"Well, c'mon in and let's talk about it."

Just as they turned to walk into the foyer, Alex heard a man's voice calling from behind her, "Hello? Hello? Excuse me."

She spun around to see a man in a suit minus the tie, running across the street toward them.

"Hello. I see you have a room for rent," he said, sounding winded. His nostrils flared in and out, but he continued to smile.

"Oh," Marguerite said with a wave of her hand in the air, "we're all set. I just need to take down that sign."

The young man's face fell, "Oh, okay then," and stepped around toward the street and walked off.

She's already decided that I can have the room?

Hank closed the front door behind Alex, and Marguerite opened the door to her apartment. Then she strode to the living room and retrieved the cardboard sign off the sill. She turned and called from down the hall, "Would you like a scone, Alex? I made them this morning."

Alex's shoulders relaxed even more. What a difference from just a few minutes ago.

"I'd love one," she called out making her way to the kitchen. It was easy to find—follow the sweet smell.

"Aren't ya' gonna ask me if I want any?" Hank barked out.

"Oh, Hank. When did you ever need an invitation for food?"

A snicker passed Alex's lips. She couldn't help herself. The banter between the couple amused her. She wondered how long they were neighbors.

"Sit here, dear," Marguerite pointed to a chair across the blue Formica table. "So where are you from, Alex?"

She sat and Hank took the chair at the head of the table. The delightful scent in the air almost distracted her.

"Well, I grew up in Kingston, but after college I moved to Los Angeles for acting. I just came back last week, and I'm staying with my brother in Soho. I was out yesterday and today looking for a place to live."

"Kingston, huh? Nice town," Hank said matter-of-factly.

"So you'll do some acting here, I suppose?"

"Yes, ma'am. My plan is to find a flexible job so I can go on calls and auditions." She glanced down at the plate of scones and the pitcher of lemonade Marguerite set down in the center of the table. "Honestly, after the luck I had yesterday, my prospects of housing or a job were looking bleak. And I'm a little nervous because my furniture arrives Thursday." She wrinkled her nose at the thought.

"You have furniture?"

"Yes." Alex waited to hear from Marguerite if that was a good or a bad thing.

"Take a bite of the scone." She did. Sweet and tasty; it melted in her mouth. "Are you feeling better? The color is back in your cheeks now."

Alex swallowed. "I do feel better. Thank you." She bit her lips between her teeth. "The main reason I left LA was because I was attacked on the street one night coming home from work." She wasn't sure why she disclosed her story to them except that it felt right. Inexplicably, she trusted them.

"Oh, dear," Marguerite said as she sank down in a chair across from Alex.

"I'm fine. But it's made me hyper-aware I guess. A panicked feeling came over me as I walked down your street, so I guess that's why I froze out there."

"That's certainly understandable," Hank said, his voice low and his eyes soft.

"Well, I'm glad we were around." Marguerite murmured as she covered her warm hand over Alex's. "Now how about we show you the room." Marguerite stood as she smiled and tucked in her chair. "The building is three stories. I live in the first two."

"Yeah, right," Hank muttered as he rolled his eyes.

Alex bit back a smile, and Marguerite chose to ignore the comment.

"So the third floor is all yours," Marguerite continued as they climbed the wide, hardwood steps. "It isn't furnished, which is why I asked you about having furniture. Utilities are covered including basic cable." She opened the door and Alex followed her in.

The space was enormous; it seemed bigger than her apartment back in LA. It was one big open space with a few half-walls dividing the living room from the kitchen. The front wall was almost exclusively windows. Alex took a few steps to check out the view and loved what she heard, the sound of hardwood floors. Her place in LA was tiled everywhere—wall to wall. She visually placed her furniture in the space: the sofa, armchair, two tables, a bookshelf, TV and room for doing yoga and Pilates.

This place had the most amazing feel, Alex licked her lips and willed herself remain calm.

She strolled to the kitchen, her hand gliding on the sparkling countertops. It held everything she needed including a full-size refrigerator and a little pantry closet, which Alex couldn't help but open. The squeak of the door broke the silence, and Alex had to smile.

"Oh, looks like I need to grease that door," Marguerite said with a bit of surprise in her voice.

"Over here, of course, is the bedroom, and this door here is to the bathroom," Marguerite pointed.

Alex peeked around in both spacious rooms. *Could it be this easy?* Chances were good this place was out of her price-range. It felt so right, so perfect.

"Um, how much are you asking, Marguerite?"

The lady disclosed the rent plus the security deposit. *Seriously?* Alex could handle that. What a stroke of luck.

"I'll take it Marguerite," and she held out her hand to the woman. Marguerite shook Alex's hand and smiled back.

"Excellent."

Alex felt dizzy with glee. Marguerite hadn't indicated that not having a job would hinder her chances for getting the place.

"Oh, and this door leads to the back stairwell, back door, and your porch, which has a washer and dryer."

Alex followed her out the back door and glanced at her little closed-in porch. Wow, Alex thought, a front-loading washing machine.

She felt at home already; it was comforting and disconcerting at the same time. Entering back into Marguerite's kitchen, she stepped toward her purse, which was slung over the chair back, and pulled out her checkbook.

"My furniture is due to arrive on Thursday. Will that work for you?"

"Certainly. You can see the apartment is vacant. It's all yours." Then she placed a one-page application on the table in front of Alex. "Just bring this back with you. I'll be here, and I'll give you a key then."

"What? You don't want me to fill this out now?" Alex furrowed her brows. She couldn't quite believe Marguerite didn't want to check references first.

"I'm sure everything will check out just fine." She leaned down and jotted her phone number on the top of the sheet. "Call me if there is any change."

"Um . . . okay." She bit her lip and looked up from her check writing. "Thanks, Marguerite. Thanks, Hank. I appreciate everything."

"You're welcome, dear."

Marguerite walked her to the front door and said goodbye.

Making her way back to Aidan's, her steps were sure and her chin high. Alex relished a lightness she hadn't felt in some time. She took a deep breath, and little giggle slipped passed her lips.

As she walked, her stomach growled. That was a good sign—being hungry. *Wow! One o'clock already.* She walked a few blocks and ducked inside a deli. The smell of beef and sauerkraut hit her the second she pulled open the door. Welcome home, Alex, she thought and ordered a loaded, calorie-packed Reuben. She'd earned it.

As she settled into a booth, she shot a text to Gloria and some of her other LA friends. She knew it would be hard to maintain a friendship cross-country, but she had cultivated incredible friendships she didn't want to blow off. In the middle of her lunch, her cell phone rang.

"Hello?"

"Hi, Alex. It's Preston Murray."

"Hey, Preston. How's it going?"

"Good. Listen, I know it's short notice, but I'm wondering if you're free tonight would you like to go out to dinner with me?"

Wow! That was quick, she thought. "Sure. I'd love to."

He asked if she liked sushi and mentioned a restaurant in Midtown he wanted to try. She gave him Aidan's address, and they agreed on a time. She disconnected the line and smiled. She dug back into her loaded and delicious sandwich. She crossed her legs and noticed her leg swung on its own volition. She grinned again. What a good day!

CHAPTER SEVEN

"HEY, SIS," Aidan said as he draped his jacket over the back of a kitchen chair. "How's it going?"

"Hey. I had a great day," her smile hard to contain.

"Really? What happened?" he said with one brow raised.

"I found the most awesome apartment. This lady in the Village owns it. I almost passed it by."

"Really?" he grinned at her.

"Anyway, this nice lady owns a three-story apartment building, and she's renting me the third floor. It's one big open space with a bedroom and a bathroom. It is an older, quaint building. I love it."

"Sounds like luck was on your side. We need to celebrate," he reached in the fridge for a bottle of white wine. He pulled down two glasses from the cabinet, poured and handed her a glass. "To a fresh start."

She grinned. "To a fresh start."

"So you look nice. What's going on?"

"I have a date."

"Cool. Who is he?"

"Interestingly enough, I ran into him Sunday at a coffeehouse and yesterday at a deli. He called me today and asked me out for tonight. We're going to Midtown for sushi."

"That sounds fun. What time will he be here?"

She knew why he asked. Aidan wanted to check out Preston personally, as if she wouldn't go out with him if he didn't meet Aidan's approval. Alex smiled to herself. She glanced at the clock.

"He should be here in about thirty minutes."

"Great. I'd like to meet him. I have some work to do, but I'll come out soon." He left for his office.

The doorbell rang fifteen minutes later. *He's early.*

Alex opened the door to a handsome looking Preston. He wore tan pants with a white shirt and a navy blazer. She had to chuckle to herself. She wore a navy dress for her date. Seeing the pair of them made her think of couples that would coordinate their outfits, like Brad and Angelina. She topped-off her ensemble with accessories and only one-inch heels so she didn't risk towering over him.

"Hi. Come on in," she smiled.

"Hi Alex, you look beautiful," he said.

"Thanks." She closed the door behind him. "Give me a second, I'll introduce you to my brother."

She walked back to Aidan's office and found him on the phone. He met her gaze and she pointed to the front door, he shrugged. Clearly, this call was too important for him to break away.

She simply mouthed *I'll see you later.* He nodded and waved.

"Maybe you can meet him later. He's stuck on the phone."

"Sounds good. Shall we head out?" he held the door open for her.

They grabbed a cab to the restaurant and were seated almost immediately. Conversation generally flowed well; only a few times did it feel strained. He asked too many questions giving Alex hardly a chance to learn much about him. And she thought it curious that she hadn't noticed how his upper front teeth seemed to crowd a bit forcing some to overlap.

Wrapping up dinner, they agreed to walk for a while. Midtown exuded energy. Lots of hustle and bustle, towering skyscrapers and, of course, Times Square. Apparently, Preston worked in Soho—that's why they ran into each other twice—although he lived in Battery Park.

After thirty minutes, he hailed a cab and took her back to Aidan's.

At the door, he held her hand. "I had a great time tonight, Alex. Can I see you again?"

Ah, the moment of truth. Did she want to see him again? The date ranked eight out of ten, so it was good although not great. *Be real, Alex. How many* ten *dates have you had?*

"Yeah. That would be nice," she conceded.

He smiled and slowly leaned in to kiss her, giving her an opportunity to turn and present a cheek. She wouldn't. She needed to know how his kiss would feel.

Soft lips, that was good. His tongue felt a little on the thick side. She'd rate it a seven out of ten.

Truthfully, Preston just didn't give her the warm fuzzies. He was more than polite and respectful, and, of course, inquisitive wouldn't be considered a *bad* trait. So for now she would reserve judgment and go out with him at least one more time.

"Good night, Preston. And thanks again." She ducked inside, only then realizing she should have invited him in to meet Aidan. *Oh well. Next time.* For now, Alex looked forward to climbing into a comfy bed for the next eight hours or so.

She entered the apartment to find her brother and Cole sitting in the living room watching sports on TV.

Her breath hitched. She hadn't expected to see Cole. All reason seemed to go awry when she was around him. Her body reacted to Cole as if he weren't gay and wondered if anybody else noticed.

It would be considered bad form to drool over your brother's openly gay best friend. Not to mention rude. She needed to pull her shit together.

They both turned to look at her as she closed the door.

"Oh, hi guys. How's it going?" *That sounded light and airy.*

"Hey, sis. How was your date?"

"It went well. So what are you guys watching?" she asked as she stepped behind the sofa.

"New York versus Seattle," Cole said nonchalantly.

"Who's winning?" She didn't know why she asked; she didn't care. Why was she stalling?

"The Yankees," her brother replied.

"Good." She placed her hand on his shoulder. "Well, I think I'm gonna hit the hay. Do you need anything out of the bedroom?"

Aidan scanned the room quickly, then looked up at her, "Nope. I got everything."

"Okay, well, goodnight."

She turned and, in a subconscious move, her fingers gently touched Cole's shoulder as she passed behind him on the way to the bedroom. A zing of electricity shot up her fingertips and wiggled up her arm. With her other hand, she squeezed her fingers together. *What was that?*

"Goodnight," they both called.

***

The next day, Cole opened his email at the spa to see pictures from Lauren taken from the top of the Eiffel Tower. They were impressive.

Looks like she had someone snap a few pictures with her too. Cole smiled thinking about Lauren trying to chat with her limited French. Knowing Lauren, she'd find a way; she was too much of a people person.

Cole stepped out of the office to make a swing through the spa. Almost everyone had a client with them. He strolled to the reception desk and checked the appointments for the remainder of the day. Nothing noteworthy with the exception of a new client who was due in mere minutes.

Cole would make sure she felt at ease so that she would continue to come back.

After checking out Mrs. Skudris, Cole heard the chime and did a double take at the front door. Alex? He blinked. It wasn't her. But she sure looked like Alex. Damn if his heart didn't jump like the night before, when Alex strolled in from her date wearing a blue dress. She rocked that dress. It took all his strength to maintain his composure.

"Hi. I'm Vicki Anderson. I have an appointment for a manicure and pedicure at one o'clock."

"Hello, Miss. Anderson." Cole stuck out his hand remembering to give a light handshake. "I see this is your first time to L'Eclisse. I'm Colton, the manager here. Why don't I give you a quick tour before your treatments?"

She smiled brightly at him. "That would be nice."

They toured around, Cole telling her about the many services they offered.

She halted and looked up at him. "You offer acupressure?"

"Yes, we do."

"I love acupressure. Another spa I went to had a fantastic girl, but she left some time ago." Her smile faded as her eyes traveled off to the right like she was trying to think of something. "What was her name? Beatrice? Bethany? Oh, I can't remember."

"Could it be Becky?"

"That's it." Her eyes beamed.

"Well, I'll introduce you to our acupressurist. I think we may be talking about the same person."

They rounded the corner to the west part of the spa where Becky stood folding towels.

"Becky?"

She looked up and smiled broadly. "Vicki. Oh, my gosh. How are you?"

Cole let the ladies chat and reconnect for a while; then he redirected Vicki to her manicure and pedicure chair.

"Colton. I will need to make an appointment for as soon as possible with Becky."

"Yes, ma'am. I'll be sure to remind you before you leave. Now enjoy. You're in good hands." He gave her a quick wink and strolled back to the reception desk.

Good work. One more new client, he thought. It always looked good to increase sales under your watch.

***

Wednesday morning, Alex met Aidan in the kitchen while he poured a cup of coffee in a portable mug. Aidan made the best coffee. She needed to get his secret to replicate it on her own. Definitely.

"Morning, sleepyhead. What's on your agenda today?"

"I'll be looking for an agent. And probably looking for any cattle calls off-Broadway or off-off-Broadway." She pursed her lips together.

"So tell me. How *did* your date go last night?"

"Honestly, it was good. The guy's nice enough, but I don't think we have much chemistry." *Like I could have with someone like Cole.* Now that was a startling thought.

"Alright. Well, I'm heading out. Got a big day." He stopped mid-way to the door. "Oh, tomorrow Jade and I are taking you out for dinner, or we can bring it by your new place. Whatever you want."

"Oh, wow. Thanks."

He smiled and headed out.

Alex pulled out a mug and added some agave and milk to her coffee. She thought about Aidan's question. She hadn't given much thought to Preston or their date. And the fact that Cole had popped into her mind right then surprised her. She closed her eyes and took a deep breath. He might be gay, but someone like him would be a good match for her. There was no denying it, Cole got her blood going in a way that Preston didn't.

Crap! That didn't mean she secretly lusted after gay guys, did it? *Nah.* That was just weird.

Cup in hand, Alex headed to the kitchen table with her tablet. She heard of some good places to search for an agent in the area, so she'd start there.

Three hours later, she had left six messages with agents, successfully booked two appointments with two others and added four cattle calls she'd like to go on for the following week.

Alex rolled her shoulders. Sitting for long periods didn't work for her. She needed to move. She changed into shorts and sneakers and headed out to the bustling city below. She made a few passes around the block at a good clip and then stopped at a deli for a chicken salad to take back with her.

Aidan's apartment was located on the fifth floor. She decided to bypass the elevator for the stairs. She had just unlocked the door when her cell rang.

A local number.

"Hello?" She panted in the phone. In hindsight, she should have let it roll to voicemail.

"Hello, Alex. This is Ralph from Peachy's. Is this a good time?"

"Yes, sir . . . er, Ralph. Just climbed a few flights of stairs that's all. What can I do for you?"

"I called to offer you a job. Are you still looking?"

Alex pumped her fist in the air once. "Yes. Yes, I am."

"Great. Can you start Friday? In fact, you'll be our Girl Friday." He chuckled at his own joke. "You'll work most Fridays and some Saturdays, depending on the time of year. Initially, I can't give you a lot of hours, but come fall you'll have as much as you want."

"That sounds great, Ralph."

"Okay. Then come by Friday about five. We'll get the paperwork going and I'll introduce you to the others. Remember to bring your social security card with you."

"I will. And thanks." She smiled big.

Alright, he couldn't promise her a lot of hours at first. Alex sucked in her cheek and bit down. She did a quick calculation of her savings. Chances were good she'd be okay, but soon she'd need to sit down and tweak her budget, keep herself on track.

Next item on the agenda, touch base with the movers.

She hung up the phone, tapping a pencil against her lips. The movers already had her new address but they didn't think they could make it to her place before noon. That wouldn't leave her much time for unpacking and organizing. *Whatever.* She'd take whatever she could get.

In need of a shower, Alex stripped in the bathroom. From the bedroom, her cell phone dinged alerting of a text message. *Dang!* She skipped to her phone and glanced. *Oh.* It was from Preston.

Just wanted to tell you I was thinking about you and I hope you have a good day, sweetie.

Leaving her phone on the nightstand, she stood straight. She didn't know whether to think that was sweet or creepy. Her lips pressed together. He might be feeling more for her than she was for him.

* * *

Alex jumped out of bed Thursday with a smile on her face. Moving day.

She quickly showered, threw on some old clothes, packed her suitcases, and carried them to the kitchen.

"Wow. You're raring to go," Aidan said with a hint of amusement in his eyes.

"Yes, indeed. I can't wait for you to see the place. Here," she slid a card across the counter to her brother. "This is my address. Come by anytime. I can't wait for you to see the place, and I can't wait to meet Jade. I'm on the third floor, so ring that bell okay?" Why did she feel like a motor-mouth?

Aidan chuckled. "Okay, but I'm probably gonna call first to see how things are progressing."

"Yeah, that's a good idea," She poured herself a cup of hot coffee, like she needed the caffeine.

Marguerite seemed just as excited to have Alex move in as Alex was. She handed her a slip of paper listing the front door keypad and a key to her apartment. Alex passed over her application and deposit in exchange. Now it was simply a matter of waiting for the movers.

She headed upstairs with her luggage and looked around the big empty space. Then, because she needed something to do, made a list of groceries to stock her cabinets and fridge. She looked out the window, waiting for a sign of the moving van. Then a knock at the door caught her attention.

"Hey Marguerite."

"Hi Alex, I know you probably don't have anything up here to eat. Would you like to join me for lunch?"

The gesture warmed Alex to her core.

"Yes, I'd love to." She slipped the cell phone in her back pocket and followed her landlady downstairs. "Marguerite, you can call me if you need me for anything. You don't have to climb all these stairs."

"Oh, I know dear, but it's good exercise."

And she was right.

Alex felt too nervous to eat, but knew she'd need her strength for the day. Her cell phone chimed interrupting their lunch. Preston. He said he hoped she'd have a good moving day. Geez! This guy was getting a bit clingy. She replied with a simple "thank you".

Not long after, the movers called. Finally. They were going through the Holland Tunnel and expected to be at her place within minutes.

"The movers are a few minutes away," she announced, feeling the rush of adrenaline hit her veins. She gobbled down the last of her sandwich and helped clean up.

Then turning toward Marguerite, she cleared her throat. "I'm going to wait outside."

"Okay, dear."

She shook out her hands, and restlessly she looked up and down the street. Finally, the van came into view.

The driver hopped down from the rig.

"Hello, Alex, this your place," he jutted his chin toward the apartment building.

"Yup, that's me on the third floor."

"Alright, well, if you could just prop open the doors, we'll get started." He and his partner each carried a box up first to get a lay of the land, as it were. "Nice place." Then he turned for the door. "Let's do it, Joe."

All in all, it didn't take too much time to get the truck unloaded. Alex didn't have that much. She gave her furniture a once over, not that the pieces were antiques or expensive, but if there was serious damage, it would be best to know now. She signed the documents and the movers were on their way.

Now it started to feel like home.

After a few hours of unpacking boxes, her cell beeped. She saw a text from Aidan.

Hey! Jade and I were thinking about dinner. Do you want to stay in or go out?

She replied:

Stay in plz. I'm on a roll. You guys in the mood for pizza?

Aidan responded quickly:

Sure, sounds good. Be there in about 30.

She realized it was after seven o'clock. She was getting hungry. She texted one last request.

Make mine gluten-free plz. ☺

True to his word, Aidan and Jade were at her door in thirty minutes. She raced downstairs to let them in. These stairs *were* going to be a good workout!

"Hey, guys. C'mon in."

Aidan introduced the slender redhead beside him. She had sparkling, deep honey eyes and plumped burgundy lips. When she turned, Alex caught a glimpse of her tiny, stud nose ring. Alex barely got the door closed when Jade pulled her into a big bear hug.

"It's so great to finally meet you. Aidan has told me so much about you."

"Thanks. It's great to finally meet you, too. C'mon up. I'm on the third floor."

They walked into her sunny apartment filled with furniture, boxes, and bare walls.

"Nice place," Jade drew out the words as she sauntered around. "You totally lucked out finding this place."

"Yeah, sis. This apartment looks good, seems to suit you," Aidan said as he set the pizza boxes on the table.

"Thanks, guys. So far, I'm digging it. I think I have a few solid hours of work and my boxes will be unpacked. Then I can start decorating."

"So are you hungry?" Jade spun around with a smile on her face. "I was so surprised you asked Aidan for gluten-free. I swear I'm the only one in Manhattan that eats gluten-free," she chuckled out loud.

Alex couldn't help herself; she laughed too.

"Well, it's a big thing out in LA. I think people finally realized the wheat changed years ago, and it's making us fat," she mentioned as she pulled out some plates and napkins.

"Exactly. So," Jade pushed the bottom pizza box to Aidan and popped open the top box, "you can have your jacked-up pizza, Aidan. Alex and I will eat the healthy stuff." And settling into a chair, she yanked a slice out of the box and smacked it on her plate.

Aidan chuckled. "Yup, bring on the *real* stuff. I'll leave you with the cardboard crap."

"So you lived in LA for a few years. How was that?" Jade asked, not waiting for an answer. "I heard it's a sunny slice of hell, where the whores walk the streets and run the entertainment industry. Where fake people clog the highways and the gangs clog everywhere else."

Um . . . what was the question again? Alex unsuccessfully bit back a smile.

"Yeah, there's some of that, but there's also great restaurants and beaches too," she said as she tipped her head and raised a brow.

"Oh, cool," Jade replied pragmatically before reaching for another piece of pizza.

"So what do you do, Jade?"

"I'm a graphic artist. My company was contracted to do some super-simple project for Aidan's company, and that's how we met," she grinned looking his way.

Aidan rolled his eyes. "Want another beer, babe?" he asked and popped the cap off a beer bottle before handing it to her.

Aidan had himself a fireball. Jade was unique but sweet, a mix of high-energy and laid-back. Perhaps, she was a bit opinionated, but not to offend. Alex decided she liked the woman and most importantly, Alex was happy as long as she made Aidan happy.

Cleaning up after dinner, Alex heard her cell phone chime. A text. And she had a distinct feeling of who it would be. Preston.

This guy is trying way *too hard.*

"Oh, I almost forgot," Aidan announced bringing her out of her reverie. "Here," he pulled a box out of his cargo shorts pocket, and handed it to her.

Her heart leaped. Her ring from Gloria. She took it and ripped off the paper wrapping.

"Thank you so much, Aidan." She slipped it right on. How a piece of metal could mean so much—be so sentimental—she'd never understand. Her eyes became foggy so she blinked quickly.

"You're welcome. So can we help you with anything before we take off?"

She looked up at her brother and bit the inside of her cheek. "Actually, there is. Could you hook up my TV?"

"Oh man," he said with some exaggeration. "What do I look like? Tech Support?"

"Actually, yes."

He threw his arms up and spun around to her media stand. The women chuckled. Her brother was a good man.

CHAPTER EIGHT

IT WAS FRIDAY, and there was no sign of Mrs. Prestavich. Cole walked out of the office to the reception desk.

"Gretchen, have we heard from Mrs. Prestavich?"

She peered up from behind the monitor and scrunched her brows together.

"Yes, she called and rescheduled for next week."

"Thanks. Let me know if she calls again, will you?"

"Sure, Colton."

Cole turned to make the rounds of the spa and smoothed a finger over his eyebrow. He told himself he was worried because Lauren would be worried. Well, worrying was a wasted emotion at this point. He would just wait to see how next week played out.

Before lunch, he shot an email to Lauren, and before he could head out to grab a bite, his foreman called him on his cell.

"Hi, Bob. What's up?"

"Cole, you need to get over here to the Reid's." Bob spoke is such a low tone, Cole almost missed what he said.

"Why? What's going on?"

"She's throwing a conniption over the tile. I mean, she's seriously pissed, and you're the only one who can calm her down."

"Alright. I'll be right there."

Cole and his team were supposed to be on the tail end of a bathroom remodel in Lincoln Square. The Reids had made so many change orders it was getting ridiculous.

He strolled out to the front. "Gretchen, I have a project I need to go check on. Do you think you and Andrea can hold down the fort?"

"Absolutely, Colton. When do you think you'll be back?"

"Shouldn't be long. An hour tops."

"Great."

Cole hustled through the building's lobby and out the door to hail a taxi. As luck would have it, one had just pulled up, letting another passenger out. He hopped in and gave the driver the Reid's address.

Mrs. Reid was definitely hot under the collar. He could hear her yelling at poor Bob through the front door. He rang the bell and waited.

"Cole, I'm glad you're here," she started. "We've got a big problem. My decorator says she doesn't want the mosaic for the shower up this high." She walked and talked and assumed Cole would follow her. Cole was used to customers like that, and he'd just let it roll right off his back.

He looked at the shower while the tile guy stood there practically shaking in his boots.

"Mrs. Reid," Cole said as he stepped into the shell of the shower and pointed to the plumbing for the diverter valve. "If you want the mosaic accent lower, we can easily do that. I'll have Saul take down a layer of travertine and put the mosaic there. But look right here. This is where your diverter valve goes for the hand-held sprayer. If I go lower, I'm afraid we'll interrupt the clean lines of the glass mosaic." He watched as she processed what he said.

Meanwhile, back at the spa, the owner, Regina Skorpio, waltzed in unannounced. Gretchen's eyes flew open, and Andrea jumped up to greet her at the door.

While Andrea gave her an update on business and appointments, Gretchen texted Cole the code for if and when Regina were to pop in: *WWW 911,* which stood for Wicked Witch of the West emergency.

Cole felt his phone buzz in his pocket. He discreetly silenced it and continued.

"Of course, I'll do whatever you and your decorator want," he said turning his palm up.

"Well, . . . I don't think she considered how big that valve or handle, or whatever, was going to be."

"Yes, well, it has a four-inch trim kit with it. That means a four-inch circle of hardware will be smack dab in the middle of your mosaic."

"Oh my, I definitely don't want that. Well, let's keep it as it is right here. I'll call my decorator and make sure she's on board. Thanks, Cole. I appreciate you running over here on short notice."

"No problem, Mrs. Reid." She walked him to the door.

"Bob, can I speak with you a moment outside?"

They stepped out into the hall, and Cole closed the door behind him.

Bob didn't waste a minute. "Cole, I swear I told her the same exact thing that you just said," he said in a loud whisper.

"I know. Look, don't worry about it. Sometimes, they just need to hear it from more than one source to make sure it's the right thing. I'm a little concerned about Saul. He looks five minutes from running for the hills. See what you can do to calm him down, otherwise just wrap it early."

Looking down, Bob nodded and then lifted his head to face Cole. "Okay, sounds like a good idea."

The phone rang in his pocket.

"Okay, you got it from here?"

Bob nodded, and Cole made his way to the elevator. "Hello?"

"Cole? It's Lauren."

"Hey, Lauren. I'm about to go into an elevator. If I drop you, I'll call you back."

"Okay. So how's it going?"

His phone chimed in his ear again. *Shit. When it rained, it poured.*

"Good. How about you? How's everything going in Paris?"

"Fabulous. At first I was overwhelmed, but I'm getting in a groove. I'm making progress on the house, a room at a time. Cole, she has a ton of photo books," her voice dropped an octave. "I'll bring them back. You may like to look at them."

Cole was so thankful he hadn't dropped the call in the elevator. He had a feeling he knew what those photographs were. His parents.

"Yeah. That would be good. So what's going on now?"

"Painters and landscapers are here now. I've got help to do some cleaning. And the real estate agent plans to put the house on the market on Tuesday."

As he stepped outside, he hailed a taxi to head back to L'Eclisse.

"How are things otherwise in Paris? Your photos from the Eiffel Tower were awesome. Who took them?"

"Well, this is a great city—so much to see and do. I hope I can take more of it in before I have to leave. And to answer your question, the person that took those pictures is a photographer. His name is Andre." Her voice sounded a hint softer, and that had Cole curious.

"Ah. So are you and Andre going out?"

"We have, yes. And we probably will again."

Cole's eyes narrowed. Based on Lauren's reply, he had a feeling he shouldn't probe too much more on the subject. For now.

"Well, be careful, would you?" He was more than a little concerned about his sister, especially with some stranger in a foreign land, where he was powerless to help her.

"I will. I better go," she said.

"Okay, take care. I'll talk to you soon."

"Love you."

"Love you back."

The timing was perfect since he had just walked into the spa to see Gretchen and Andrea looking completely panicked.

"Ladies, what seems to be the problem?"

"Colton," Andrea started, "didn't you get our texts or voicemails?"

Gretchen stood. "Regina's here," she said in a stage whisper. "She's in your office."

"It's okay. Thanks for trying to get a hold of me," he turned to make his way back to the office and the hostile crackpot. The truth was, despite the calm exterior, he didn't know what to expect with this little confrontation. Based on the girls' reaction, Regina was on a warpath.

He smoothed a hand over his hair and cleared his throat. Opening the door, Regina sat at his desk, and her eyes met his ready to shoot daggers.

"Hello, Regina," he said smoothly.

"Don't *Hello Regina* me! I've been waiting for you. Where have you been?"

Here goes.

He took the seat across the desk and casually crossed his legs. "I'm glad you came in today. It saves me a call."

"You were going to call me? Oh, pray tell." Her voice dripped with condensation. She crossed her arms.

"I came from a meeting with . . . let's say, a reliable source that claims we could have some not-so-friendly competition in the area."

Regina's brows didn't furrow, probably because of the Botox, but her eyes read confusion.

"What do you mean?"

Cole reached behind him to push the door closed, then leaned closer to Regina and said, "There is a . . . rumor that says Catalonia could be moving blocks away from here.

Regina sat straight in her chair and sucked in a breath through her distended nostrils.

"Don't worry. I'm on it. I understand it's all very preliminary, and they are looking at other locations as well. I'll keep you posted with what I hear." With that, Cole leaned back in his chair and crossed his legs, resting his hands in his lap.

"I don't like this one bit," she stated through clenched teeth. "I'm glad you got wind of this early. I hate surprises, Colton. Do you hear me?"

"Oh, I agree." *Not in the least.*

"If they move into our territory, they better get out their checkbooks, because I'll make them bleed."

The woman was vicious. He merely kept his mouth shut and nodded.

She sat and thought for another few moments, eyes darting. Cole sat and waited it out, feeling the slightest trickle of sweat down his neck.

She stood suddenly, so Cole stood as well. "Keep me posted, Colton."

"Yes, ma'am."

And she stormed toward the door, barely getting out a goodbye to the ladies.

Crisis averted.

The back office line rang.

"I'm okay."

"Oh, thank God." It was Gretchen.

"Anything else I should know? Anything about her visit I should be aware of?"

"No, Colton. She did mention something about the sales staying strong even though you were in charge. Sorry."

Cole laughed, and it felt good. "No, that's okay. I appreciate you trying to reach me. I had

Lauren on the other line. I'm going to get some work done back here for a while. Let me know if she returns."

"Will do," Gretchen disconnected the line.

Cole pulled out his cell and there it was in blue and white—Gretchen's 911 text. He laughed again. When he came up with *WWW 911*, he certainly didn't think they would need it. It's not that Regina would necessarily dislike Cole being pulled away on remodeling projects, she didn't want to know about it. At least that's how Lauren described it.

God, how he missed his sister.

She'd come home with all kinds of stories about the clientele or the employees, which usually made them laugh over dinner. Once in a while, Lauren would complain about something Regina said or did but, for the most part, regarded Regina as a smart business woman.

That's why Cole had been prepared.

He had decided on day two of this escapade, that it would be better to have a back-up plan for instances like this when Regina decided to pop in. After a week, he'd tell her everything dissolved for fear the rival spa would lose too many clients in the move.

Of course, he'd have to come up with another tall tale to save his ass. He rolled his eyes.

CHAPTER NINE

ALEX SHOWED UP her new job a few minutes before five. She found Ralph right away.

"Hey, Alex. Why don't you follow me to the back office? We'll get the paperwork out of the way, and then I can introduce you to the others. Most everyone will arrive at six. The band goes on at nine. Sunday through Thursday the band will go on at eight since we close earlier."

Ralph gave her a tour of the bar. She could see some detail from the building as it was originally made, like older light fixtures, chair rail, some exposed pipes, and chipped subway tile. That, in addition to the dark hardwood floors and high ceilings, made the place comfortable and welcoming.

Ralph showed her the break room with lockers for storing her stuff. He mentioned random drug testing, which didn't bother Alex and frankly, she completely expected it. Then, she took a seat at his desk, and he handed her a waist apron.

"You don't have to wear this, some girls like it. We have no uniform here, just a dress code. No shorts shorter than your knuckles when your arms are straight down, and no shirts that reveal too much cleavage."

"Okay."

Without him saying so, Ralph was trying to run a respectable establishment and Alex couldn't be happier.

He went on. "If you're gonna be late, just let me know with as much notice as you can. If you need time off, same thing applies. You can swap shifts with another server if you need to, but tell me if you do. You will never close the bar alone. About once a week you will be scheduled for an on-call shift. And you can have a drink at the end of your shift, on the house." He paused and pursed his lips, thinking. "Any questions?"

"No, sir. I think that covers it for now. If I think of something, I'll ask."

"Great. Let's go meet the motley crew."

They moved from the office to the bar where folks already started to gather.

"Hey Eric. Sasha. Come meet our Girl Friday."

Sasha strolled over and rolled her eyes blatantly.

"Hi. I'm Sasha. Girl Thursday."

Alex couldn't help but giggle. "Hi. I'm Alex."

"Hi. I'm Eric. I mostly tend bar."

She shook both their hands. "Good to meet you."

Ralph pointed to another woman serving a couple across the bar. "And that's Dottie. You'll meet the rest of the crew tonight and tomorrow."

"Great, thanks."

"Sasha, want to give Alex the lay of the land?"

Alex tied on her new black apron and followed Sasha around the bar. Alex had a good feeling about working in this place. Ralph created an open atmosphere built on respect, and she liked that.

A steady flow of customers came in over the next couple of hours, and Alex got into her groove right away. Not having worked for a few weeks, she was concerned she might be rusty.

That night's band was a throwback eighties band, and they were good. They played everything from Billy Joel to The Police to Kiss. The energy in the place spread like wildfire, and the drinks flowed like water. Alex did consider what the noise would do to her hearing, but she was having such a good time, she'd table that for another time.

As the band took their second break of the night, Alex spun around to head to the bar and almost ran into Preston.

"Oh my gosh! Hi, Preston. How are you?" *What is he doing here?*

"Hi Alex. I'm great. How are you doing?"

She stepped around him and made her way to the bartender to get an order filled.

"I'm good. Just a little crazy right now." She wiped her brow with her shirtsleeve.

"I can see that. This looks like an awesome place. I can't believe I've never been here. Mind if I sit at the bar for a while?"

"No, make yourself comfortable. Eric's the bartender. He can get you a drink." Then she pointed at Eric, like Preston wouldn't figure that out on his own.

Alex caught a flash of something in Eric's eyes. Maybe confusion? But just as quickly, it was gone. Her forehead wrinkled.

"Hey. What can I get for you?" he smiled to Preston.

"I'll have a Manhattan."

What? That's what my parents drink, she thought. Then before she could say something rude, she smiled at Preston, grabbed her tray of drinks and headed to her awaiting customers.

The band returned, and the volume in the place shot up. Preston remained seated at the bar. To his credit, he didn't bug Alex at all. He knew she was working her butt off, not to mention it was her first day on the job. Perhaps she judged him too harshly this week?

After his second drink, he stood and met up with Alex while she waited for Eric to fill a drink order.

"Hey, I think I'm gonna head out now. This is a really cool place to work, Alex."

"It is, isn't it?" she smiled.

Then placing his hand on her waist, he leaned in and gave a soft, slow kiss on her cheek. Behind his shoulder, Alex got a glimpse of Eric watching them as he shook a drink.

***

Saturday late morning, Alex continued organizing her apartment and trying to make it feel like home, when she heard a knock at the door.

"Hi, Marguerite."

"Hi Alex. How's everything going so far?" she asked as she followed Alex into her apartment. "Looks real nice."

"Yeah, thanks. Things are coming along. What's up?"

"Oh, I usually do a big meal on Sunday nights and I wanted to ask if you'd care to join me and Hank for dinner tomorrow."

She smiled inside. The way Marguerite looked out for her warmed her heart.

"Yes, I'd love to. What can I bring?"

"No. Nothing. Just bring yourself. Drop by around six, okay?"

"Sure, that sounds great. Thanks again." What a pleasant surprise. She had the night off, so partaking in a delicious home-cooked meal would be perfect.

Alex arrived at Peachy's a little before her shift started. She didn't have to close, but she'd work late. Eric and Nasrin, a beautiful Persian woman with a great smile, were in the backroom chatting.

"Hey, guys."

"Hi, Alex," they both called out.

"So, I've been thinking about this, and I'm curious. Was the bar always called Peachy's or did Ralph name it that?"

Eric and Nasrin looked at each other. Nasrin turned toward Alex. "Ralph named it after his wife. It was her nickname."

"Was?"

"She died a few years ago. The idea for this bar was hers. Ralph's owned this place for over a decade," Eric told her.

"Wow." How very sad for Ralph, Alex thought. "How'd she die?"

"Breast cancer."

"I think we're all working until eleven," Eric changed the subject. "How about we check out that new bar in Tribeca afterward?"

"I'm in," Nasrin said with a smile on her face.

"Sure. Why not?" Alex chimed in.

Peachy's was hopping. The band had a female lead singer that night which seemed to draw a bigger crowd. Alex got into her groove—the tips piled up, and the customers seemed to be having a good time.

Only one thing could deflate her bubble, and as she whirled around to return to the bar, she saw him. Preston. He made eye contact smiled and waved.

Shit! Him again.

Approaching his seat, she said, "Hey, Preston. I'm sorry but I'm not going to be able to talk much today. We are slammed."

"Oh, I know. I sent you a text earlier. Maybe after your shift I can take you out somewhere?"

She gave her order to Eric. "I'm sorry, but a few of us are going out afterward. It would be good for me to join since I'm new here."

He glanced down and moved his glass in his hands. "How about tomorrow or tomorrow night?"

He sounded so hopeful, and she didn't want to lead him on. One date had been enough. "Sorry, I can't then either. I have tons to do, and then I have dinner plans."

"Oh, I see."

She loaded her tray of fresh drinks to deliver to her table, and caught a glimpse of Eric rolling his eyes.

She had to give Preston an A for persistency. She might think differently of his advances if she liked the guy. But his smothering behavior began to grate on her. It was time to cut bait.

***

Overall, Alex had a great weekend. Tips on Saturday were great, which meant she could buy a pair of new sunglasses she'd been eyeing.

Hanging out with work friends afterward turned out to be surprising. Nasrin brought her boyfriend with her, which made the night feel awfully similar to a double date. The situation made Alex uncomfortable and after about an hour she excused herself and took a cab home.

The downside to her weekend had been Preston. *Poor Preston.* He called her and texted her no less than four times on Sunday. He wanted to go out again. She didn't reply to any of them. Hopefully he would take the hint.

On Monday morning Alex started her search for a new talent agent. Her first meeting was with a woman from a mid-sized firm. Based on their conversation, the agent had a lot of experience placing actors like Alex in some excellent roles. However, on a personal level, they didn't seem to connect.

Now, she was in the waiting room of an office of another talent agent, Paul Blanchard. Flipping through a magazine, she heard a voice calling her name.

"Alex?"

"Yes. Hi, Paul." Alex stood.

He held out his hand, and Alex shook it.

"Please come into my office. Can I get you something to drink?" Paul asked before closing his office door.

"No, I'm good. Thanks," she smiled.

"I got your resume and photos. What brings you back to New York?"

Alex had rehearsed her answer to that question, leaving out the less-favorable details, and Paul seemed to accept it. He asked about her schooling and acting experience. She highlighted her accomplishments and special talents. He asked her "show me what you can do," and she pulled out one of the monologues she brought to audition.

Then she quizzed him about his role and knowledge of the local industry. He owned his own firm and strove to keep it that way because by being small it meant "more attention and pushing harder" for his clients.

Her first impressions of Paul were positive. He seemed relaxed and laid-back, but also incredibly focused and determined. She liked that. She also liked his business philosophy.

"Alex, I want to check out your references, but you should be hearing from me in the next day or two."

She agreed but had a good feeling about Paul representing her. They shook hands and said their goodbyes. Alex walked outside and upturned her face, smiling at the sun. She knew she wanted to work with Paul. She only hoped he was willing to take her on.

CHAPTER TEN

BUSINESS AT THE SPA stayed constant most of the day, with the girls taking calls for appointments leading up to the fourth of July. A minute before Cole decided to grab lunch in the back office, Densi Parker walked in.

In Cole's opinion, Densi wasn't the typical confident client at the spa. She kept quiet and to herself most of her time there. Cole wondered if something traumatic had happened in her life to bring about this quiet, shy nature.

One thing that struck him though was her fascination with shoes. Lauren once told him that Densi would look at shoes online while sitting in the manicure chair. Last week, Densi had brought with her a change of shoes for after her pedicure. Today, Cole noticed she had on a pair of simple strappy heels that gave her calves strong definition.

"Good afternoon, Densi."

"Hello, Colton." Her gaze dropped down to her hands grasping her handbag held in front of her.

"I couldn't help but notice your fabulous pumps."

She peered down and her head popped up with a smile on her face. This might be the first time he'd seen her full smile.

"Thank you," she said softly. "They're Manolo's 'Chaos Cuff'. I really like the silver buckle. Last year's had a gold buckle." Her white teeth no longer showed, but the smile loomed and her eyes sparkled.

"Oh, wonderful. I can see why you bought them. Well, let's get you started, shall we?"

Cole strolled back to his office. He was getting the hang of this gay stuff, and it was only the beginning of week two. Over lunch, Cole shot Lauren an email telling her about Regina getting her feathers ruffled, but how quickly he smoothed them for her.

Surprisingly, Regina made him grin. She had a tough exterior and liked to put up such a front, but Cole knew deep inside lived a human scared of failure.

Next, Cole called Ace about possibly getting together. Ace was spending more time with Jade as of late—and Cole was cool with that—but he wanted to make a concerted effort to keep their friendship strong.

"Hey, Cole. How's it going?"

"Good, man. I'm calling because I wanted to see what you're up to tonight. Maybe we can go grab a beer."

"Yeah, that sounds great. Oh, wait. Alex wanted to hang tonight. I guess she's got the night off and is feeling stir crazy. Care if she joins us?"

"No, that'll be fine." Nope. No problem at all as far as Cole was concerned. He enjoyed spending time with Alex. She had an energetic and funny side that he found quite entertaining. As long as she thought of him as gay, there would be no problem whatsoever.

"Great," Ace said. "I got another question. It seems my dad has a hernia."

"Oh shit."

"Yeah. I guess it's not terrible, but the doc wants to do surgery Wednesday. I spoke to my mom, and she's little stressed about it."

"I can imagine."

"She's concerned he'll try to do work himself. I'm planning to head up there Friday night and see what I can get done over the weekend. Any chance you can break away from the spa?"

"Sure, absolutely." Cole knew Lauren occasionally took Saturdays off, and since the spa was closed on Sunday, he knew he'd have a solid weekend to help out.

"Great. I appreciate it, man. Let's meet at Bar None around seven."

"Roger that. See you there."

***

Alex, Cole and Aidan sat in a laid-back bar in Soho drinking margaritas and munching chips with salsa.

The place appeared to have undergone a renovation recently. The wood floors and tables gleamed. The walls were painted a cool gray. And the coolest thing of all—a pale, blue-gray Lucite bar that was lit from underneath. It seemed to be a great gathering place for after work because the joint was packed.

"How's the unpacking going?" Aidan asked.

"Pretty well. I'm slowly getting settled," she replied. "My stuff is fitting, it will just take a little time before it feels like home. So, Cole, are you coming up to my parents' farm this weekend?" Alex asked as she glanced his way.

Being around Cole, Alex had to admit, felt awkward. The man sat next to her in a snug t-shirt and jeans. He leaned back on his chair, his chest and arm muscles on display. Even his smile was to die for. He looked good, too good, and it was turning her on. Her body came alive in his presence and all she wanted was for her hands to explore every square inch of that glorious body. But, he was gay! How in the hell does she tell her body to mind her brain?

"Yup, that's the plan. Any work we can do, means something less your father will need to do himself. Will you be there, Alex?"

"Yes, but I have to work Friday night, so I'll take the train up on Saturday morning." She turned to look at Aidan. "Let me know when you guys are heading back on Sunday, and I'll get on the same train."

"Sure."

Alex scanned the crowd when the sight of a man coming through the door caught her eye. She spun around in her chair, eyes wide. She turned her back toward the door as much as possible.

"Shit," she said through gritted teeth. Her heart jackhammered in her chest.

Aidan furrowed his brow and asked, "What is it?"

"The guy I was seeing just walked in. Crap!" Geez, how could she get away from this guy? Seriously!

"And I take it you don't want to see him," Cole assumed with a hint of sarcasm.

She turned back to see if her ex—not that you could call him that since their dating was short-lived—had noticed her. He definitely had. In fact, he stood on his toes to get a better view over the throng of people collected at the bar. Then headed her way.

Alex pivoted back to Cole, let her head fall back and let out a big, jovial, flirtatious laugh. She brought her head straight, leaned forward putting her hand on his knee and laughed some more.

"Ace, I think something is wrong with your sister."

Both men looked at each other, frowning and looking truly puzzled.

Continuing to smile, Alex murmured through her teeth, "Please, Cole, do me a favor. I know I'm asking a lot, but pretend that you're my boyfriend. Please. Pretend to be straight."

Moving only her eyes, she glanced to the right and saw her ex moving closer to their table. She grabbed Cole's hand off his thigh and jumped on his lap, wrapping his arm around her waist.

Looking almost paranoid, Alex met Cole's gaze head-on and still smiling said, "Laugh. Pretend like I just said something funny."

A smile may have been on her face, but panic and desperation filled her eyes. So, Cole threw his head back and let out a deep laugh. Alex laughed and swung her arm around his shoulder placing her hand on his back. She tipped her head toward Ace and eyed him. Some sibling communication arched over the table because he started to laugh too.

Alex turned back to face Cole. She stopped laughing and licked her lips. She glanced down at his lips then back to his eyes. Shit! She planned to kiss him.

Her warm lips came down over his softly, gently testing. Her hand moved up the back of his neck and cupped it. She slowly swiped her tongue along the seam of his lips.

He could do this. She needed a "boyfriend". *She thinks you're gay.*

He slid his hand from her waist down to cup her ass. He took his other hand to the back of her neck and held her. He thrust his tongue in her mouth. Her mouth was soft, warm and sexy. She felt amazing in his arms. He savored the reverberation of her moan in his mouth, which shot straight down to his dick.

Shit! Abort. Abort.

He pulled back to break the kiss and caught a glimpse of her glazed, softened eyes. He didn't know if she had sensed anything unusual with him.

"Alex," he heard from overhead.

Alex twisted on Cole's lap to look up at a young Kiefer Sutherland.

"Oh, hi, Preston," she said sounding slightly breathy. "How are you?"

He furrowed his brow at her, "I'm good. How come you never returned my calls?

"Oh, geez, Preston. I'm so sorry. That was rude of me. My old high school flame," she smiled tilting her head toward Cole, "called me out of the blue, and well, you know what they say about sparks never dying out."

"No, I don't," his lips thinned to a frown. *Buck up, man. She's not into you. Time to move on.*

"Again, I'm really sorry."

The man stood there, looked at Cole then at Aidan, like he expected one of them to come to his rescue or something.

"Well, I'll see you around," he turned to leave and head to the bar where his friends waited.

Alex drew in a deep breath and exhaled. She turned to face Cole and in a low voice said, "Thank you."

She slid over onto her chair. Ace leaned forward placing his forearms on the table. "What the hell was that about?"

"I met the guy shortly after coming back to New York. He seemed nice enough and we went out on a one date. But the guy started getting too clingy, maybe even obsessed. I hadn't quite figured out how to tell him to take a hike, but when I stopped returning his calls, I figured he got the message, and I was off the hook."

"Until now," Cole said.

"Until now," she replied. "And thanks again. The next round is on me."

"Hmm." Cole eyed her but didn't say anything else. He could only show disapproval, knowing he felt the exact opposite. That might have been the best damn kiss he'd had since Rebecca Whitehead his freshman year in college. Maybe even better than Rebecca.

Damn! Cole grabbed his bottle of Heineken and chugged the rest of it down. If the beer didn't work, he'd need a flipping cold shower.

Cole and Aidan walked her home around midnight. Alex couldn't help thinking about Cole and their kiss. It felt so *real*! She wondered if he had kissed a woman before because that felt phenomenal. She fibbed to Preston about Cole being her rekindled love boyfriend, but how she wished it were true. Cole was undoubtedly making some guy very happy.

She considered asking Aidan more about him, but why bother? It'd be like going down the candy aisle when you're allergic to chocolate—wanting and wishing things were different.

* * *

Tuesday morning, Alex rushed down the street to an old, eighty-seat theater in Greenwich Village. She hated to be late. She took a deep breath to calm her panting before signing in.

She read about the cattle call for a minor part in an off-off-Broadway play and thought she'd give it a try. She didn't know if she was exactly what they were looking for, but most times these things were about playing the numbers. The more calls you go on, the more likely you are to land a part.

That afternoon, she called Paul and spoke to him for a few minutes. She had a good feeling about him, and really didn't need to look anymore. She crossed her fingers.

"Well, I'd like to represent you if you're still interested, Alex," he said.

"Yes." She knew her enthusiasm streamed through the phone.

Paul chuckled. "Alright. Great. First things first. I'll email you a contract. Sign it and send it back to me. In the meantime, I'll do a search on my end to see what pops up. Keep an eye out on email because I may get wind of something, but won't call you if it's late."

"Okay. I can do that."

"It will probably be small stuff in the beginning, Alex, but stick with me, and I'll bring bigger jobs your way."

"Okay," she smiled because she believed him.

CHAPTER ELEVEN

MRS. PRESTAVICH walked into the spa so quietly that Cole wouldn't have known she was there if not for the chime at the door. She arrived ten minutes early for her appointment.

"Good morning, Mrs. Prestavich."

"Good morning, Colton. Is Deanna ready for me?"

"Nearly. Why don't you have a seat, and I'll bring you a cup of herbal tea?"

"Thank you. I appreciate it."

Cole hustled to the back and returned with a fresh cup of herbal tea on a saucer. Instead of handing it to her and returning to the reception desk, he took the seat next to her in the waiting area.

"Thank you." Her voice sounded congenial, but the air of depression and sadness clearly evident.

"Mrs. Prestavich," Cole started, "Becky has a new type of massage she is trying out in the spa, and I'm wondering if you would be willing to give it a try—complimentary of course—and provide us some feedback?"

She looked up from her cup, her eyes subtly aglow.

"It's called Foot Zone Therapy. It's like acupressure and very recuperative."

"Um, that sounds interesting. How long does it take?"

"Only about twenty minutes."

"Yes, I think I have time for that," she said.

Cole glanced up to see Deanna now free. "Hello, Mrs. Prestavich. Are you ready?"

Mrs. Prestavich and Cole both rose. "Deanna, Mrs. Prestavich will be having another service when she's done. If you could please take her to Becky, that would be great."

"Sure thing, Colton."

The two ladies walked toward Deanna's room. Already Mrs. Prestavich seemed to be holding her head a little higher. When she canceled her appointment last week, Cole knew he had to do something for the woman. He had overheard Becky talking about Foot Zone Therapy to Gretchen, and he considered that could be just the answer. So Becky had kept her calendar clear for the timeslot and happily agreed to help. Cole took a deep breath and returned to the desk to review the remainder of the week's appointments.

After about an hour, Mrs. Prestavich met Cole at the desk.

"So, how did everything go, Mrs. Prestavich?"

"Positively wonderful. If the foot massage becomes a regular offering, I would like to have more," she smiled. Then she handed him her credit card to pay for her Botox.

"I'm glad to hear that. Just remember we're here for you when you need to escape for a while. Everyone needs to get away sometimes."

She glanced up, paused, and gave him a small, knowing smile. "You are so right. Thank you for the treat."

"You're very welcome." And with that he watched as she gracefully pivoted on her heels and glided out the glass spa doors to the elevator.

After an early lunch, Cole made his way to the reception desk to relieve Andrea for her lunch. Mrs. Fulton arrived shortly after that. She looked about Cole's age with short, curly brown hair and an outgoing personality.

"Hi Colton. How's it going today?"

"Hello, Mrs. Fulton. I'm fine. How are you?"

"I'm super. I have a question for you before I go for my massage," she said as she rested her forearms on the counter, her eyes bright. "I have a brother, Roland, that I would like you to meet. I think the two of you would get along famously."

Oh fuck. She was fixing him up. *Shit!* He hadn't planned for this.

"I know how blind dates can be," she continued. "How about I give you his number? Then you guys can talk, and if you like him well enough, you can go out," she said with a hopeful tone in her voice.

"Sure, that sounds fantastic." He plastered a smile on his face, and she handed over the paper with Roland's number on it.

"Terrific. He's looking forward to hearing from you."

Margie sauntered to the desk and greeted Mrs. Fulton. "You ready, Mrs. Fulton?"

"You bet," and the ladies left.

Cole glanced down at the paper in his hand. *Crap!* He shoved it in his pants pocket. How the hell would he get out of this one?

***

That night at work, as Alex got ready for her shift, Nasrin walked into the backroom.

"Hi, Alex."

"Hey, Nasrin."

"Call me Nasy. You closing tonight?" she smiled brilliantly.

"Yes. You too?"

Nasy nodded.

"So your boyfriend seems nice. Have you guys been dating long?"

Opening a locker, Nasy smiled and turned to face Alex. "Yes, a little over a year."

"Awesome. It was nice that he could join us Saturday night."

"I know, right? He's working on his Masters, and I was certain he'd want to study, that's why I didn't even bother to ask him."

Alex froze. "I'm sorry." The woman had her confused.

"Oh. I mean, Eric prodded me to call him and invite him out with us," Nasy said as she tied her apron on. "I didn't think he'd say yes, so I was surprised. Sorry you had to leave early."

"Yeah. Me, too."

Nasy smiled. "I'll see you out there," she pushed open the break room door to head to the bar area.

Hmm. Eric told her to call her boyfriend to join us. Her eyes narrowed. It wasn't her imagination—it was meant to be like a double date.

Alex mentally shook her head. Perhaps she was reading too much into it. Eric might just be the kind of guy who believes the more, the merrier. She grabbed her apron, tied it around her waist and closed her locker door.

Business for a Tuesday night seemed constant. Hopefully, it will stay like this through the summer, Alex thought. She looked forward to the tips. They were the holy grail of any waitressing job.

When she strolled up to the bar to give her table's order, she saw Sasha.

"Hey girl," she called. "How's it goin'?"

"Hey, Sasha. It's real good. I'm getting into a groove. This place seems like a good place to work."

"Definitely. And Ralph is the best," she smiled.

"You closing?" Alex asked.

"Yes. You too?"

"Yup. Okay, I'll talk to ya'," Sasha lifted her tray of drinks to take to her table.

Eric loaded drinks on a tray for Alex. "How are you, Alex?"

"Good, Eric. How are you?"

"Good. Did I hear you right? You're closing tonight?"

"Yep."

"Darn. I was thinking of hitting the movies and thought you'd like to tag along."

"Oh, sorry. Maybe next time." *Crud.* She hadn't meant to say that. She in no way hoped for a next time. Honestly, Eric wasn't her type. He seemed like a nice enough guy, but she could only see him as a friend. Plus, there was something unusual about him, something she couldn't put her finger on, which made her uncomfortable.

She balanced her tray and swiftly made her way to her customers before Eric could start asking *when* they could go out.

After waiting on customers for about an hour, Alex spotted Aidan and Cole walking into the bar.

"Hey, guys." She hugged her brother and then Cole. What a handsome duo. "What brings you by?"

"Hey, Alex. Nothing much. Just thought we'd come in and check out where you work," Aidan said with a smile.

"Well, I'm glad you did. Take a seat over there, and I'll bring you a couple beers."

Cole and Ace watched Alex wend her way to the bar as they took a seat where she directed.

Glancing around, Cole noted, "The bar has a good feel."

Ace nodded. "Yeah, it does."

They got comfortable at a round table when Alex brought them two Heinekens. "Let me check on a few tables, and I'll be right back."

Cole watched Alex bop around to her customers' tables, to the bar, and back again. He noticed her chatting with the bartender and another waitress. They all glanced at him and Ace, and he got the distinct impression they were the topic of discussion.

After several minutes, Alex approached their table with two women. "Guys, this is Sasha and

Dottie. Aidan, my brother, and Colton," she motioned to the men.

They stood and greeted the women. "Hello. Nice to meet you both."

"Nice to meet you too," Sasha smiled. "You arrived at the perfect time. The band will be on in about ten minutes."

"Excellent," Ace grinned.

"Well, I better get back to it. I'm behind the bar tonight," Dottie proclaimed and shook their hands.

"I should leave too. Go check on my tables. Good to meet you both," Sasha smiled and shook Cole's hand, then Ace's. "Come in anytime," she said while looking at Ace.

Alex grinned as she watched Sasha walk away. The men returned to sitting. "Aidan, I think Sasha might be interested in you." She looked at her brother with a chipper smile.

"Yeah, yeah," he said as he rolled his eyes and took a big gulp of beer.

Alex chuckled and spun away from the table to head back to her customers.

Cole and Ace sat and watched the band perform their first set. During the break, Alex brought by another co-worker.

"Aidan, Colton. This is Eric, one of the bartenders."

"Hi," Ace stood and shook hands. "Good to meet you."

"Hello." Cole gave a nod and shook his hand, bearing in mind not to make it too firm.

Eric had two longnecks in his left hand and set them on the table. "Here you go, gentlemen. On the house."

"Thanks," they both replied as they sat.

"Well, Aidan, your sister is doing a bang-up job here," he said as he placed a hand on her back and rubbed. "Everyone likes her," Eric said with an overly enthusiastic smile on his face.

Cole noticed a gentle shift in Alex's posture. She seemed uncomfortable with Eric touching her. The thought made Cole wince inside.

Ace looked up at Alex and nodded. "Excellent. She's always been a hard worker." Alex smiled a closed mouth smile at her brother.

"So, you tend bar?" Ace asked, focusing back on Eric.

"I do," moving his eyes from Ace to Cole and back. "I'm done though. Now I get to enjoy the rest of my night."

"Care to join us?"

Eric paused momentarily then declined. "I'm good. You guys enjoy. The band is about to come back on."

"Thanks again, man," Ace said holding up his beer bottle an inch.

"You're welcome." The men shook hands, and before Eric turned to leave, he said to Alex, "Have a good night."

"Well, you seem to work with some nice people, Alex," Ace observed.

"Yeah, I think so," she gave a little nod, but her eyes looked unconvincing, like she had something more to say. "Well, the band is back and I need to make my rounds. I'll catch you guys in a while." She flashed her pearly whites and left the table.

Cole leaned forward toward Ace and said, "I do get the impression Eric makes her uncomfortable. Like he's too touchy-feely for her liking."

Ace glanced up at Alex across the room and pursed his lips. "Hmm. I guess, I didn't notice."

Well, Cole had, and he wasn't thrilled with the idea. He took a big swig of his beer and rocked the bottle on the table for a moment. Alex was Ace's baby sister. That meant he had a responsibility to look out for Alex too. Absolutely.

CHAPTER TWELVE

THE NEXT MORNING, Alex got ready for an audition. She learned from Sasha about a casting opportunity for a national commercial for a painkiller brand. Alex, then mentioned it to Paul, who was able to get her an audition time for the next day.

The train dropped her Uptown, two blocks from where she needed to be.

Commercial castings generally didn't take much time out of her day, which was a good thing since she had plans for the evening with her brother, Jade, and Cole. She arrived, signed in for the audition and took a seat beside another woman, who appeared close to Alex's age and with the similar long, dark hair and big eyes. She looked like one of the great movie stars of the forties.

"Hey."

"Hey."

"Are you here for the painkiller commercial?"

"No. Nail polish," the woman grinned and nodded.

Alex glanced down at her hands. "Wow, you do have nice hands. And nice nails."

The woman lifted her hands an inch off her lap. "Good genes," she stated frankly. Then she looked up at Alex and smiled. Alex chuckled and shortly they both were laughing.

"Alex Marshall," she held out a hand.

"Yolanda Herrera. But you can call me Yoli."

Geez. Alex had to admit, her name alone sounded like a movie star. "Nice to meet you, Yoli."

And before their conversation could continue, Yoli was called in for her audition.

"Good luck," she called to Yoli.

"You too," she smiled back.

After another ten minutes, Alex was called for her audition. She briefly met the casting associate, then the director who gave her a run-down of the setup. The roll asked for a fitness-minded woman who would jog in Central Park, stop for the camera, read her lines into the camera, and continue on her run. Alex wore athletic shorts and a t-shirt and pulled her hair into a ponytail, so she definitely looked the part.

"Any questions?" the director asked.

"No. I'm set."

Alex did her slate for the camera and showed her right and left profiles. Then she read her lines, which were sent to her the prior day.

Then they tried the scene with the run added in. Alex smiled to herself. She believed she gave the director what he asked for, and it felt good. Afterward, she waited for any additional direction or feedback.

The associate raised his brows and nodded slightly.

"I like it Alex. The right amount of enthusiasm and sincerity." He nodded again. "Okay, you'll be hearing from us in a day or so."

"Great. Thanks," she spun around to leave.

On her way out to the hall, she noticed Yoli waiting for the elevator.

"Hey. How did it go?"

"Oh, hi, Alex. Good. I think I'll at least get a callback. You?"

"I think it went well. You never really know what they're looking for though." Alex rolled her eyes.

Yoli chuckled. "True."

Entering the elevator, Alex thought about Yoli and the potential for friendship. "Do you work another job?"

"Yes. I temp," Yoli replied.

"I wait tables at Peachy's in Soho. If you're ever around, stop in."

Yoli smiled. "I will. I know the place, but I haven't been there in quite a while." As the elevator came to a stop, they walked through the lobby together. "I'll be sure to stop in and see you."

"Excellent. Well, it was great to meet you," she said lightly.

"Great meeting you. I'll see you around," the woman waved as she proceeded down the sidewalk.

Alex waved back. That's what she needed more of in this town—friends. Oh shoot, she thought, we should have exchanged phone numbers.

***

Aidan, Cole and Alex ordered another round of beer, and Alex plopped her feet up on the chair beside her. She brought the bottle to her lips and took a swig.

An evening off, when she could be waited on for once, was a glorious thing. But if she ran into Preston again, she'd spit nails.

Turning her attention to Cole, "So, how is work going, Cole?"

"Oh, you know. Another day, another dollar."

"Isn't your sister supposed to come back and take over running the spa again?"

"Oh sure, but not for another two weeks."

"Are you not enjoying it? I mean, the money working in the Upper East Side must be very good, yes? Surely it isn't hard labor?" She smiled.

He grinned. "No, it isn't hard labor, and yes, the money is good. It's taking some . . . getting used to. But overall, I like it. It's a great spa and the girls I work with are super."

"Hmm," she nodded.

That slight nagging feeling Alex had in the pit of her stomach came back. Something didn't quite feel right with Cole. Nothing sinister. More like . . . off.

Perhaps he could read the questioning look in eyes.

"What?"

She squinted and shook her head slightly.

"I don't know. You don't . . . I don't know," she stammered. Perhaps she shouldn't finish. She didn't want to offend her brother's best friend. Not to mention, a really decent guy.

"What?" he asked again.

"You just don't seem very gay." There. She blurted it out and felt the heat rise in her cheeks.

Aidan spat some beer and coughed. They both turned to look at him.

"Sorry," he said, cleaning his chin.

"Well, how does someone *seem* gay?" Cole asked, his eyes momentarily wide.

"Oh, I don't know. Forget I said anything." *Shit.*

"Alex, let me ask you something. Do you think a straight guy knows the difference between a French manicure and an American manicure?"

She snorted. "You work in a spa." The implied "duh" hung between them.

"True." He pursed his lips, uncrossed his legs and leaned closer to her. "But does a straight guy know the difference between this year's Manolo's 'Chaos Cuff' and last year's? Does a straight guy know to hang a drapery rod all the way to the ceiling while making sure the drapes touch the floor? Does a straight guy know how to pronounce Hermes?" he said drawing out the Z-sound at the end. "Hmm?"

Double shit.

At that precise moment, Jade walked in and planted a big, loud smooch on Aidan's smiling lips. "Hi babe. Hi guys. Sorry I'm late. What did I miss?"

"Hi, Jade," Alex said giving her a half-smile and pulling her feet off the chair to the floor.

"Hello, Jade. Love your hat," Cole said of her straw cowboy hat sporting a faux turquoise stone in the center.

"Thanks, Colton. So seriously, what did I miss?" She turned to Aidan knowing he would fill her in.

"Alex doesn't think Cole is gay."

Jade looked at her. "Really?"

"Yeah, but I'm probably wrong." She could see Cole nodding from the corner of her eye.

"Well," glancing between her and Cole, "we're all bi-sexual anyway, so it hardly matters." She twitched a shoulder then browsed for a waitress.

She made that statement as if she had done nothing but comment on the weather. Eyes went wide, and Alex's mouth gaped. The waitress approached the table, and Jade ordered a beer.

"Anyone need anything else?" the waitress asked.

Aidan looked up at her, still in shock, "No, we're good." Then he looked at his girlfriend. "What do you mean, 'we're all bisexual anyway'?"

"Yeah?" Alex narrowed her eyes. Jade was no dumb redhead. She was a smart cookie, but the woman had some, perhaps, squirrely views on life. *This,* Alex had to hear.

"Well, just that." Jade looked at the group. "Physiologically speaking, men and women are quite similar. One could argue we have more in common, than we have differences. So these hard and fast rules that define men and women become very gray at times. Especially times of high emotion, like lust, for example."

The waitress returned and set Jade's beer down. She took it and tipped her head back, swallowing a gulp. Again, she sounded nonchalant like she didn't set off an explosive at the table.

The three stared at her in disbelief, and she knew it.

Jade exhaled audibly, dropped her elbow on the table and waved her fingers beckoning Alex.

"Look. Come here."

Alex thought she wanted to arm wrestle, which confused the hell out of her, but she placed her elbow on the table and grasped Jade's hand. Jade gently jerked Alex's arm, pulling her closer to her. Then with her free hand, she smoothed the side of Alex's face and pushed her hair back. Alex felt nervous, uncertain of what to expect.

"Relax, I'm not gonna hurt you."

Then with her fingertips only, Jade glided over Alex's face and throat. It felt like a light massage, so good. Maybe she should blame the three beers she drank. Her natural inclination was to close her eyes, and she did. After just a beat, she felt warm lips gently brush over hers. Jade held her head still and continued the kiss. Lightly, her lips and tongue glossed over Alex's lips. She parted her lips slightly, and Jade slid her tongue inside. Alex gave up; she couldn't help herself. She felt Jade tilt her head to give her a full-blown tongue kiss. She tasted of beer and something sweet. Someone moaned.

Who knows how long the kiss lasted. Sweet, soft and warm. Jade finally pulled back, looking at Alex straight on. Alex slowly opened her eyes and took a moment to refocus. She knew her face flushed; she felt overly warm.

"Be honest. You're wet aren't you?" Jade asked confidently.

"Um . . ."

Jade raised her eyebrows.

"Maybe a little," Alex said in a whisper glancing down at the table.

Jade leaned back in her chair grabbing her bottle for a drink. "I rest my case."

Aidan slid his chair closer to Jade, grabbed her face, kissed her cheek and—although he may not have known Alex could hear—he whispered in her ear,

"That was fucking hot. We need to get out of here now."

Alex didn't know what to feel. Mortified would be good for starters. She tipped her head over to glance at Cole, who had his eyes pinned on her. *Shit.* She brought her hands up and hung her forehead in them. But when she looked down, she couldn't help notice Cole's pants seemed stretched across the front. *What?*

Cole leaned forward close to her face. "You alright?"

She peered at him. Should she say something to him about his obvious semi? She opted to wait. She plastered a simple smile on her face saying, "Yeah. I'm good."

Aidan rose flipping cash on the table. "Hey guys, we're gonna head out."

"Sure thing. I'll talk to you tomorrow, Ace. Have a terrific night you two."

Jade stood. "Take care, guys." Then, looking at Aidan, "C'mon stud. Let's see what we can do about that stiffy you're carrying." She took his hand in hers and they were off.

"Alex, that was freaking crazy." Cole looked at her in awe. Perhaps that was something he'd never seen before. "Are you alright?" he asked again.

She took her elbows off the table, took a breath, sat taller and looked over at him. "Yeah. That was crazy, wasn't it?"

He raised an eyebrow. "Hell yeah. Any straight guy would have a lifetime of fantasies having witnessed that girl-on-girl kiss."

"Seriously?" She was mortified, but he thought it was hot.

He simply nodded. "C'mon. I'll walk you home."

"You don't have to do that. Your place is close. And I'm all the way in the Village."

"True, but you've been here, what? Two weeks? I don't want you getting lost. Not to mention, a gentleman never lets a lady walk home alone. Let's go."

Gentleman, huh? Alex's wheels were turning. Her gut told her Cole wasn't gay, and the evidence mounted. Soon she would put her theory to the test.

After several minutes of walking, chatting along the way, she and Cole arrived outside her apartment building. She punched in her code and pushed open the heavy door when she heard it unlock. She kept it propped open with her foot. Cole stood beside her, watched and waited. She kept her left hand on the door and reached to place her right hand on his chest. She smoothed it over his cotton shirt feeling his solid chest.

"Thanks so much for walking me home, Cole." She leaned forward and kissed his cheek. But she didn't stop there. Her lips moved down his cheek to the corner of his mouth, then dead-center on his lips. A soft kiss on his warm, firm lips. Slowly, she smoothed her lips over his. His lips parted slightly, and she slipped her tongue through and gently touched the tip of his. He parted his lips a fraction more and Alex slid her tongue into his mouth, caressing his tongue. He didn't pull back, and when Alex felt his tongue stroke hers in-kind, she decided not to hold back. She swept her hand up his muscular chest and cupped the back of his neck and tilted her head to take the kiss deeper.

The kiss was pure delight. In all the years of kissing, this one definitely ranked in the Top Ten. She felt the moisture gather at the apex of her thighs. She moaned.

At that moment, she felt Cole flinch. Then he reached up and pulled her hand down. She pulled back. He stared into her eyes. She saw for the briefest of moments fire and passion in his gorgeous emerald eyes. Quickly he spun his head looking up the sidewalk one way, then down the other.

When he turned back to refocus on her, his lips thinned and his nostrils flared.

"What the hell was that about?" he scolded in a gruff voice.

Oh shit! She'd awakened a sleeping giant.

She gave him her sweetest smile, then glanced down to the front of his pants, the building erection evident. He raised his head, eyes narrowed, looking about to give her a fabricated reason as to why, if he were truly gay, he would have an erection from kissing a girl. Before he could even open his mouth, she cut off his thoughts.

"Just a little goodnight kiss, Cole. See you Saturday at the farm." She dashed inside, the door locking behind her.

There was absolutely no way in hell he would let Alex walk home alone. Not after what she went through weeks before in LA. But, dammit all, when he used the term "gentleman", he knew he'd screwed up since gay men wouldn't generally refer to themselves that way. He sensed she caught it too.

Evidentially, she caught on. *Fuck!* That kiss roused and electrified. Where did she learn to kiss like that? He didn't want to go there.

All he knew was watching Jade kiss Alex at the bar set him off. He saw her eyes flutter closed and watched as her pink lips moved with Jade's. Her face started a slow ascent to red, and her nipples noticeably poked against her t-shirt. She looked enticing, and he was damn near ready to haul her away just as Ace did with Jade.

But there was too much at risk. Hell, he made a commitment to his sister and breaking that meant jeopardizing her excellent job, and possibly her reputation. She might never forgive him if he screwed it up. He had two weeks left. Surely, he could keep his dick in his pants and away from Alex for two short weeks.

He took a deep breath as he strolled into his apartment, congratulating himself on not letting that kiss go any farther. Because seriously, Alex was beautiful with her long brown hair, sparkling brown eyes and kissable pink lips. After he'd come to his senses, he panicked that someone could have seen them. The coast had looked pretty clear.

Then the thought hit him. He would be seeing her again at her parents' place upstate in two days. *Fuck!*

CHAPTER THIRTEEN

ALEX AND AIDAN'S dad was diagnosed with a hernia, followed shortly thereafter with a laparoscopic surgery. According to the doctor, their father shouldn't perform any strenuous activities until he was recovered in about three or four weeks. That proved to be difficult living on a farm. Work needed to be done—work that Alex's mother could not do by herself.

Alex took the first train out of New York to Kingston on Saturday morning. She dozed on and off during the two-hour ride. Thoughts of Cole rattled through her head. She only vaguely remembered him when growing up. At one point, she sort of recalled Aidan and Cole were on the same baseball team. Maybe because they were three years apart, they didn't socialize with each other's friends much. If Cole were gay then, she'd have no way of knowing.

Regardless, the evidence all started coming together and it made sense. Alex surmised that Lauren had to go to Paris and take care of their aunt's estate, so the only way she could do that would be to have a decent replacement for herself. And that replacement was Cole. Alex knew from conversations with Aidan that the spa was highly exclusive, attire was optional, and the clientele were only female, which explained the gay part.

Cole was probably the first and only male at the place. Who knew what skills Cole possessed that made him highly qualified, but that didn't matter. All Alex knew was that evidentially for four weeks, Cole was to act gay and fill in for his sister so that she would have a job when she returned to the states.

Interesting.

Alex's grin grew. She loved a challenge. Admittedly, realizing Cole wasn't gay delighted Alex to no end. She was attracted to Cole from the moment she laid eyes on him. She was drawn to him. The flashbacks of him eyeing her weren't merely to analyze her fashion or hairstyle, it quite possibly could have been about something more. And that "more" was just what Alex wanted to capitalize on.

"Alexandra!"

Alex heard her name called from across the train station. Her mother beamed at her and waved.

"Hi, Mom." She walked up to her mom, dropped her bag, and hugged her.

"Baby, it's good to see you."

"Mom, it's only been three weeks." Alex rolled her eyes as she smiled at her mother. "How's dad feeling?"

"Oh, he's feeling fine, but I am thankful you guys came up here. Your father is itchin' to go back to work. The boys keep trying to shoo him away. God bless 'em. You may see him at the house. Otherwise, you'll see him after he and Aidan get back from getting supplies at the hardware store."

The women walked out the front of the station toward the car, and after her mom popped the trunk, Alex swung her bag in and closed the lid.

"So what's on the agenda for this weekend?"

"The boys are working on the barn, fixing the stable doors and other repairs. Your father is repairing the electric fence." She turned toward Alex. "Thank goodness the horses haven't realized it isn't working," she said with a grin. "You can help the boys, but when you want a little sun, come find me in the garden."

"Okay, sounds like a plan."

They chatted more during the fifteen-minute drive to the farm. Her mom pulled up beside the house in time to see Aidan and her father walk out the back door.

"Hey, pumpkin!"

Alex took off her sunglasses and swung her arms around her father. "Hi, daddy."

"We are headin' out to the hardware store, ladies. We should be back in an hour or so."

"Okay," Janine said.

"Hi, sis. Bye, sis," Aidan called as he climbed into the passenger seat of the pickup. And they took off for town.

"Come on in, Alex. You can drop your bag. Then I'll give you a lemonade to take to Colton. He's probably sweating to death out there."

Alex walked out the back door toward the barn about sixty yards away. As she got closer she could hear hammering. The door was wide open, and she heard music coming from inside as well. She peered through the doorway and froze.

Cole stood shirtless in denim jeans wiping his face and neck from sweat that covered his entire body—his very muscular, tan, smoking hot body. He threw down the towel on a stool and went back to hammering planks of wood on a workbench. His muscles flexed and contracted with his every movement. He hadn't shaved, and his face stubble made him look infinitely delicious. Very bad boy.

Alex was almost breathless. She had seen a lot of chests in her day. Sometimes on the set, the male actors would need to make a costume change and would have no qualms doing so right in front of everyone. Nothing compared to the sight before her. He had practically no chest hair, just a smattering below his navel and smooth chiseled muscles. She could feel moisture gather between her thighs.

Get it together, she chided herself.

She straightened her back and, with glass in hand, walked over to Cole.

"Hi, Cole. Here's some lemonade. Mom thought you might be thirsty."

Cole had sensed he was being watched. He could see her silhouette in the doorway as he reached down for his hammer. Alex. He knew it was her—her height, her long brown hair, the curve of her hip. He wondered how long she was going to watch him until she spoke.

"Thanks," he said reaching for the glass and gulping half the beverage before taking a breath.

"Look," she started, "I owe you an apology."

"An apology. For what?"

"Well, it was inappropriate of me to kiss you the other night when you walked me home."

He sat the glass down next to his towel and put his hands on his hips. "I should say it was," he replied gruffly.

"I crossed the line. I hope I didn't make you too uncomfortable. And I promise not to say anything else about you not being gay. I can see how wrong I was."

"What?" What the hell was she implying?

"I mean, it's certainly not your decision to be gay. You were probably born that way, and I, for one, think no less of you. I truly hope we can be—"

He cut her off. "What the hell are you saying, Alex? Was there something wrong with the kiss? Even gay men kiss, you know."

"Oh, I know," her eyes going wide. "And I didn't mean to insult you. I'm sure your boyfriend likes the way you kiss."

"I don't have a boyfriend," he swallowed hard, "currently."

"Well, that's okay. I'm sure it'll happen for you. There's someone out there for everyone, right?"

He wanted to reach over, wrap his hands around her silky smooth neck and squeeze. He felt the heat rise from his gut, across his face, and out his ears. His nostrils flared. He took two steps closer to Alex. She stepped back. Her eyes going wide. He stepped even closer and had her backed up against the stable door.

He'd be damned if he let her get away with thinking his kiss was mediocre. He placed his hands on the door over her shoulders. He leaned in closer and heard her ragged breath. He reached to the side of her face and gently blew on her neck. He moved even closer and with a fingertip, hooked her t-shirt neckline and pulled it down to expose more delicious skin. He tasted her creamy skin with the smallest touch of his tongue and felt her quiver. He proceeded to gently kiss and lick her neck. He heard a little moan escape past her lips. *Good.*

He worked his kisses up her neck, to her face and then to the outside of her lips. Her face moved fractionally, wanting more. *Double good.*

He smoothed his tongue over the seam of her lips, and she parted them. He slid his tongue into her mouth and found her tongue waiting for him.

The kiss quickly turned heated and eager.

Cole let go of her t-shirt collar and moved his hands down her shoulders to the sides of her torso. Then brazenly, he grazed his thumbs over her breasts only to discover her hardened nipples. She reached her arms up and cupped her hands over his shoulders. She moaned into his mouth.

He lowered his hands to the hem of her shirt and pulled it up, exposing her stomach. This was crazy, he thought. But he couldn't stop himself. He thought about Alex for two weeks now. Clearly his body was in control, not his head.

With only the tips of his fingers, he grazed her stomach and felt her goose bumps. Then he brought her tee higher, pushing it over her breasts. His hands cupped their fullness and stroked her nipples again.

This time, he moaned.

He released her mouth and went down to her satin-covered breasts. Full, pert and waiting for his mouth. With one hand, he teased and tempted her nipple gently squeezing, twisting and tugging while his mouth sucked and played with the other. Her breathing sounded labored as she arched her back into him.

"Cole," she breathed.

He moved his mouth to the other breast and began to tease and please her in the same fashion. She writhed, whimpered beneath him, and pulled on his hair as she moaned.

He would keep this up until she climaxed. And moments later, she did just that. She let out a low cry and tossed her head side to side. Cole raised his head and saw her incredible face. He kissed her deeply and pulled her t-shirt back in place.

Slowly she opened her eyes. They were glazed over but still looking at him.

"Now *that* was a kiss, don't you think, sunshine?"

She stared at him, and as her focus returned, "Oh my God," she breathed.

He pushed back from the door slightly to give her space, only then truly realizing what he'd done. He spun around and ran his hand down his face.

"Shit," he said looking down at the dirt floor. "Fuck." He could spit fire.

He turned to meet her gaze, and she merely stared at him wide-eyed. They both faced the doorway when they heard the roar of the pickup truck engine making it known her father and brother returned.

He didn't know what to say, until finally, "I. . . I better help them unload."

She nodded and watched him leave.

That was unreal, she thought. She knew what she was doing. She intentionally baited him. She poked and prodded to get him to kiss her again. She wanted to prove to him that she knew his truth. Then she would let out a big Ah-ha!

But, . . . Oh, my God.

What the hell happened?

She crumbled under his touch. He made her come just by stimulating her nipples. *Unreal!*

His kiss, his touch, his smell. *Dear God.* She was in over her head.

Alex left through the barn's side door and, when the coast was clear, high-tailed it back to the house. She quickly changed her bra and t-shirt, and went out back to help her mother in the vegetable garden.

CHAPTER FOURTEEN

WHEN ACE HAD asked Cole to go upstate to his parents' place to work on the barn, he willingly agreed. There was never a question regarding his friend. Whatever Ace needed, Cole would give.

Besides, Gretchen and Andrea could easily handle the spa while he was away for the weekend. He and Ace took the last train up Friday night and they would return Sunday after dinner, which gave them two solid days of work. It was a good plan.

Alex, however, did not factor into that plan. When she showed up, all reason went out the window. What the hell was wrong with him? He never before had any trouble controlling his emotions or his actions around women.

This time, though, he let her get the better of him. And now he was thoroughly fucked. No one was supposed to know about his charade. If word got out, he would be fired, and more importantly, Lauren would be fired.

It was one in the morning and Cole was beat, so why was he wide awake? He'd put in a hard day's work—they all had—but instead of getting some shut-eye, he lay in bed with thoughts of Alex racing through his mind.

He reached for the sheet and flung it off. He sat up, rested his feet on the floor, and rubbed the heels of his hands over his eye sockets.

He slipped his shorts on over his boxer briefs, and headed downstairs to the kitchen for a glass of water, careful not to make a sound. From the sink, he stared out the back window.

What the hell was he going to do?

First off, he needed to talk to Alex and make her swear she wouldn't tell a soul about him, or risk bodily injury. If she even breathed a word, he would personally take her over his knee and . . .

What was that? Was there someone out there?

He squinted. Yes, there was definitely a figure, someone standing by the pond. He set his glass down and went to the back door. It was ajar. He quietly pushed the screened door and walked out onto the porch. He couldn't be certain, but it looked like Alex.

He stepped down from the porch and quietly walked toward her. There was a half-moon shining that night, and as he approached, the image became clearer—definitely Alex . . . in a bathrobe.

Her silhouette brought his senses alive—her lean legs, the roundness of her ass, the outline of her perky breasts. He would love nothing more than to touch every inch of that body and tunnel into her tight channel until she screamed his name.

"Interesting to see that I'm not the only one awake at one in the morning."

She gasped and jumped at the voice behind her. She spun around and saw Cole coming closer. Shorts and no shirt. God, did he look good. Her heart picked up pace.

She hadn't be able to sleep to save her life. Thoughts of what happened in the barn racked her brain the rest of the day, through dinner, and now, when she was supposed to be sound asleep.

They had both acted perfectly normal. No one suspected a thing. But it was all she could do not to think about it. So about half an hour ago, she got up and decided to go for a walk.

She loved the water. Standing by the oversized pond, she watched the moonlight glistening on top, beautiful. As a little girl, she would play outside and find any excuse to be by the water.

"Hey. Couldn't sleep."

He walked up beside her. "Me either. What a great night to be out," he said looking around and up at the moon.

The temperature had cooled to a very comfortable level. The sky was clear, and they could see hundreds of stars. In the distance, they heard crickets making their music. Alex took a deep breath of mountain air.

"Yeah. It sure is."

"Alex, I'll leave you alone, but when we get back to the city we need to talk about what happened today in the barn."

She turned her head to face him and stared into his eyes. What could there be to talk about? He rocked her world in a way that she'd never felt before. What did he think? She'd pretend she didn't know the truth?

Not to mention, standing this close to Cole did something to her insides . . .

"I don't want to talk about it." *I'd rather touch, not talk.* Her voice came out low and breathy. She bit her lip. Did she really just say that?

His eyebrows shot up, and as he turned to face her, he put his hands on his hips. "What the hell do you mean?"

She rotated her body to meet his gaze head-on and took one step closer, leaving mere inches between them. Her mouth felt dry. She licked her lips.

"I don't want to talk about it," she whispered.

He only stared deep into her eyes; then he looked back at the quiet house. Sexual tension electrified the air around them. Her heart beat hard against her breast.

He locked his gaze back on her, and in a low, husky voice, he murmured, "No."

"Yes," she breathed.

She would no longer deny it, she wanted Cole. There was an unquestionable energy between them. Perhaps it was only sexual, but it was most certainly strong. She wanted him, and she sensed he felt the same.

In an unexpected move, he reached up to the back of her neck, grabbed the hair that fell behind her, and yanked. It hurt only slightly, and perhaps his intent was to shock. She wouldn't give him the satisfaction. She met his stare dead-on.

"Goddammit, Alex." He plunged his lips down on hers with such ferocity, she gasped in his mouth and swung her arms around his neck, clinging to him.

He thrust his warm tongue into her willing mouth and dominated her, overwhelmed her. Her breasts became heavy, and her nipples peaked at the memory of what he could do to her body.

He slid a finger down the front of her robe to pull the sash apart and wrapped one muscular arm around her low back.

"I don't want to want you, Alex," he said into her neck.

"I know," she smoothed her hands up and slowly down his chiseled chest, that fine muscular chest that stopped her cold earlier at the barn.

He slipped her robe off her shoulders and brought his lips to her neck, kissing and licking, leaving a hot trail on her skin. Shivers tickled her skin everywhere. She moaned as he slid the strap of her cotton camisole off her shoulder.

He drove her mad with wanting. She stood before him in nothing but a cami and string bikinis, and felt over-dressed.

She glided her hands down his taut stomach, beyond his waistband to the urgent erection she felt through his shorts.

In a passionate move, he whipped both camisole straps down her arms, exposing her breasts. She gasped as his mouth lay siege to one nipple and licked. Bound, she fought to keep her hands on his firm erection, and he flexed his hips, pushing into her hands. She took one hand to work his button and zipper. She heard her breath over the crickets; she was louder. Her sex ached, and moisture saturated her panties.

She pushed her hands into Cole's shorts and caressed his silky smooth length, moisture seeping at the tip. He groaned over her breast. He sucked and tugged at her nipple.

"Please. Oh God, Cole," she breathed letting her head fall back.

He pulled back and grabbed the hem of her cami and pulled it up over her head. Her arms came back down and pushed his shorts down. He wrapped an arm around her waist, forcing her breasts against his chest. She savored the skin-to-skin contact with Cole. He kissed her passionately again, his tongue delving deeper. She felt delirious with need.

"You make me crazy, Alex," he said against her lips.

He lowered them to the ground, shook out her robe and laid her down over it. She stared up into his fiery green eyes. Then he pushed up onto his knees and slid his hands down her body, over her breasts, sending ripples through her stomach. He swirled his fingertips over her mons. She couldn't catch her breath.

He shifted and hooked two fingers under the bikini panties at her hips and slowly pulled down. She lifted her hips, and Cole continued until he flicked them off her ankles. He looked down at her completely naked and exposed.

"You have the most amazing body."

His eyes traveled up to meet hers. And without breaking her gaze, he moved between her legs, spreading them wide. The grass tickling the bottom of her bare feet.

With a single finger, he glazed over her bare sex gently. She arched her back off the ground and gasped at the sensation.

"Ah." Her voice barely audible.

"You are so wet," he said as he played over her slick opening, dragging the moisture over her clitoris. He circled over her clit making her writhe under his touch. She clenched at whatever lay under her hands—grass, robe. He was relentless.

"Do you know how sexy you look right now?"

He slipped in two fingers, and her back bowed again. The sensation was divine inside her as he pumped. She was close. He leaned over her, kissed her face, her exposed throat, and licked at her lips.

"Come, Alex. Come on my fingers."

She came, and he smothered her cries with a kiss. She wrapped her arms around his neck, and kissed him back. She hadn't even realized he'd stripped out of his briefs until the moonlight caught his silky, veiny member. She reached for him—large, thick surrounded by soft, trimmed hair. He felt marvelous in her hands, but she knew there could be more.

"Oh, please Cole."

He groaned, and she removed her hands. He slowly gently pushed inside her opening and she moaned. The exquisite feeling of Cole's hot, silky penis pushing against her walls made her want to cry. His movements were smooth and controlled. She floated to Cloud Nine.

She opened her eyes to see him looking down at her. His beautiful emerald eyes afire, the blonde of his hair catching in the moonlight.

"You are beautiful," she whispered; then pulled his head down to have his lips on hers. She wrapped her legs around him and moved with him. Flesh to flesh.

Her climax started to build again.

"Oh," she breathed against his lips. He pumped harder and pushed her to the point of no return. The sensation ricocheted throughout her body.

He caught her cries in his mouth, waited for her to finish and pumped a few more times before he pulled out and, with a groan, spurt his seed on her stomach.

He collapsed down beside her, breathing heavily.

"God, Alex."

"Mmm," was all she could say.

He lifted his body on an elbow and looked down at her. "I swear, I've never done that before."

She knew he referred to their unprotected sex. Meeting his intense gaze, she said, "I believe you."

"Stay here," he commanded before he slipped on his boxer briefs, grabbed his shorts, dipped a few inches in the pond and wrung them out. He returned to where Alex lay, kneeled beside her, and gently wiped his semen off her belly.

"Good as new," he proclaimed, tossed his shorts aside and caressed her tummy with his hand.

"It's funny," he started. "Growing up, I thought you were this giddy little girl bouncing around without a care in the world."

She turned to face him, the corner of her lips lifted.

"And I thought you were such a serious boy. Like you didn't know how to have fun or something." Her tone turned serious. "Like you had the weight of the world on your shoulders."

He glanced off into the distance. "I did."

She bit her lips together. She was touching on an extremely sensitive subject, but she couldn't stop herself. She wanted to—had to—know more about this infinitely fascinating man.

"How old were you when your parents died?"

"I was six, and Lauren was about eleven."

She felt her eyes cloud. The thought of losing her parents sent a shiver through her. Her parents meant everything to her. Sure, as an adult she understood death was a part of life, but a six-year-old boy? Unfathomable.

"Cole, I'm so sorry. I can't imagine what you went through." She stroked her hand over his cheek.

He inhaled and exhaled deeply. "Time has healed that wound."

She wasn't too sure about that. He seemed reserved and closed-off at times, and she knew it had to be because a tragedy like that doesn't merely fade away. Alex just wondered if he would ever move past this and let anyone, other than his sister, in.

He removed his hand from her stomach and said, "C'mon, sunshine. It's late. We need to head in."

He held out a hand to bring her to standing and helped her get dressed. Then he brought his shorts to the pond again to rinse off the leg. He returned to her and took her by the hand, and they quietly walked back to the house. He brought her to the threshold of her room, paused, leaned down to place a chaste kiss on her lips and whispered, "Goodnight."

"Goodnight," she whispered back, feeling bereft.

She wrinkled her brow as she watched him down the hall. But after several steps, he turned back to her. He clasped his hands around her face and leaned down to kiss her. Tipping her head, he took the kiss deeper, stroking his tongue fervidly against hers. She simply melted against him and placed her hands on his waist for support.

Then he pulled back slightly to whisper in her ear, "Sweet dreams, sunshine."

"Sweet dreams," she whispered back. And he made his way quietly down the hall to his room.

She entered her room, silently closed the door, and took a deep calming breath. "Oh, Lord above."

She dropped her robe, and a slow smile came across her face as she climbed into bed.

Absolutely amazing, she thought. Then drifted off into the best sleep she'd had in years.

CHAPTER FIFTEEN

THE TRAIN RIDE back to the city remained mostly a quiet one. Cole and Aidan chatted for a while when Cole noticed Alex against the window, fast asleep.

They worked hard this weekend. The repairs in the barn were complete, the electric fence fixed, and the garden hoed and weeded. Feeling satisfied, Cole closed his eyes for a few moments and listened to the hum of the train.

The train pulled into the station at seven-thirty five on the dot. After a short cab ride, the guys escorted Alex to her apartment building.

"Thanks, guys," she called as they watched her walk into the building and waited until she closed the door behind her.

The cabbie took off for Soho and didn't drive three blocks when Aidan asked his burning question.

"What's going on with you and my sister, Cole?"

Cole turned to glance at his friend and saw concern in his eyes. Ace suspected something. He felt Ace's irritation throughout the day, and knew Ace was merely biding his time until he could confront Cole.

"She knows."

"She knows?"

"Yup. I don't know how, but she knows I'm not gay."

Ace thought for a second and smirked. "Well, she is an actress. No doubt she recognizes bad acting when she sees it."

Cole winced, and gave him the appropriate hand signal. "I suppose you're right," he grumbled.

Ace shifted to face him. "Listen, Cole. We've known each other for a long time, so I'll get right to the point. I've suspected you two had sort of . . . ah . . . chemistry between you, probably from day one. Right?"

Cole looked at his friend and could hear the reference to *sexual chemistry*. He nodded.

"Whatever you guys decide to do about that is up to you both, but she's my sister. You're my best friend. I don't want to have to choose. I don't want to see her hurt. Understand?"

Cole read him loud and clear. He didn't blame the man. He'd have the same conversation regarding Lauren if necessary. "I understand, Ace."

Cole walked up to his building and thought of Alex for the hundredth time that day.

Damned if their previous night wasn't fantastic. *Oh shit!* Straight men did not say *fantastic*.

Whatever.

Making love to Alex was all he'd expected and more. She was hot and sexy, an incredible wet dream. He loved her boldness as she made her intentions known. At the same time, he loved how malleable she became under his touch. Damn if she didn't light up like a torch.

Shit! No way could these trysts continue while he worked at L'Eclisse. She was no one-night stand, but he had two damn weeks left. He could keep it together until Lauren returned. If need be, he would just avoid Alex for the next two weeks.

Cole shook his head recalling their conversation about his parents' death. His natural inclination was to clam up. But on some level, it felt easy opening up to Alex. There was an inexplicable safety and comfort he felt when he was with her. It was a feeling, aside from Lauren, he hadn't experienced before with anyone.

He strolled into his apartment. It was funny how quiet it seemed without Lauren around. He locked the door and made his way to the fridge to grab a beer.

He would have to call Alex in the morning. They needed to talk. The first thing to cover—no more sex until Lauren returned and he was clear of his responsibility. There was too much at risk until then. The second thing was the fact that they had unprotected sex.

He could kick himself for that move. He'd been consumed with the need to be inside her. Who could resist her breathy pleas? He lost his mind. Barely exercising restraint, he forced himself to take it slow. Only after being engulfed by her heat did he realize he was bareback.

Fuck, she was incredible. He groaned. Just the thought of her and he got hard.

***

Monday over lunch, Alex decided she needed to place a call to her beloved brother. She'd try his office line first.

"Aidan Marshall."

"Aidan. It's your sister. You know—the one you tell everything to. The one you tell your secrets to. Remember her?"

"Hey, Alex. What's up?"

Oh, he was being obtuse. "How come you didn't tell me Cole was straight?"

"Ah. I was wondering when you would call me on that."

Then the air over the phone was silent. "Yeah . . ."

"Yeah, what? I have nothing to say." She could hear him exhale. "Look, Alex, I'm sorry I couldn't tell you, but it wasn't my secret to tell. Cole is trying very hard to help out his sister and doesn't want to screw it up. Not only for the sake of her job, but considering the value of the estate. He thinks the fewer people that know the truth, the better."

She wrinkled her brow. "What does that mean? The value of the estate?"

"His portion totals one and a half million bucks. There's a lot at stake."

She gasped. *That's unreal.* "I see."

"What's happening between you two?"

"Oh, wouldn't you like to know."

He chuckled.

"Seriously, I don't have much to tell. He is noticeably focused on the spa, and that doesn't leave room for dating right now."

"Well, I definitely sense chemistry between the two of you. I hope it all works out."

"Thanks. Can you tell me, what is he like?"

"He's a good man. He's always had my back for as long as I can remember. Sometimes he holds his cards close to his vest though. But the more you get to know him, the more he opens up."

"Thanks, I appreciate it."

"Well, I'm gonna get back to work. Talk to you later."

"Talk to you later."

That afternoon, Alex returned to her apartment with a handful of much-needed accessories for her new home. She fell in love a little more every day with her cozy little pad.

As she stashed her oven mitts in a drawer, her thoughts wandered to Cole. Her weekend with him was amazing. Cole had to be the best lover she'd ever had, not that she had all that much to compare against, but nevertheless, the man was talented.

She hadn't heard from him all day, although he may retreat to Mars for a while before he tells her "never again". And he would, she just knew it. The question was how long could she go without being intimate with him? She closed her eyes and took in deep breath.

Maybe she should check her supply of fresh batteries.

She strolled into her bedroom and slipped on a tank top and a pair of old cut-offs. She didn't have to work at the bar that night so she planned to organize her things, and hang pictures and drapes.

After an hour, she stepped back to admire her work when her doorbell rang. *Wonder who it could be?* Perhaps some packages she'd been expecting.

She hustled down two flights of stairs and saw Cole standing on the other side of the door. She opened the door and almost lost it. Cole in a suit. A gorgeous charcoal suit, top button unbuttoned and his tie loosened. Dark suit, light hair, and tanned skin—what a great combination. Dear heaven above.

"Hey."

"Hey. Wanna come in?"

"Yeah, that'd be great."

He followed Alex upstairs to her apartment. He glanced around. Quaint building, solid wood staircase and banister, high ceilings. He saw several spots where the spackling had flaked off. He would love to get his hands on this place. Freshen it up, but keep it authentic.

But Goddamn, Alex's sweet ass was mere inches from his face. And in her cut-off jean shorts, he had an excellent view of creamy white cheeks.

Stay focused, he scolded himself.

They entered her apartment and took a look around. Spacious, he thought, and sunny. Perfect for her.

"Nice place."

"Thanks. I really like it. I totally lucked out finding this place, and the landlady is awesome."

He slipped off his jacket, draped it over the back of her kitchen chair and turned to make eye contact with her.

"I wanted to drop by and talk about this weekend." She didn't seem surprised by that comment.

"Okay. Care to sit?"

"No, I'm good. What happened was . . . well . . . incredible. But it can't happen again. I'm filling in for my sister, and her job is on the line if I screw up. Understand?"

She took a step closer in his direction with a smile on her face.

"What's so funny?" he snapped at her, harder than he had intended.

"I knew you were going to say that," she kept that funny smile on her face.

"I'm serious, Alex," he tried sounding serious, but the more he looked at her face, her twinkling brown eyes, the more he wanted to tan her behind, and then fuck her until she forgot what day it was.

Keeping his gaze, she said, "Cole, I'll be your Fag Hag."

"My what?" His eyes narrowed. "How the hell do you know that term?" He crossed his arms over his chest.

"I do live in The Village, Cole." She shook her head twice and smirked at him.

Silence. He cocked an eyebrow and contemplated her words. She had a point. *Ah, crap.*

"I don't know about that, Alex."

She made a step closer; he could practically smell her shampoo.

"Cole, did you not like Saturday night? Because I loved it. It was quite possibly the best sex I've ever had."

Damn straight.

"And I'd hate to just throw all that away when we have a perfectly fine working solution. What did you think about Saturday night?"

"It was good." His voice came out huskier than he'd like. His cock gave a little jump just to remind him.

"How did it feel kissing me?" She brought her hand gently to his pecs, smoothing slowly up and down.

"Good." Now his pants were stretched across the front. Another step, she closed the distance even more.

Damn, she was good.

He reached a hand to her waist—to bring her closer or keep her back—he wasn't sure.

"And being inside me? Sliding deep inside me. Hearing my cries of ecstasy. How did that feel?" She licked her luscious pink lips, slowly. His eyes fell half-mast.

She played him, and God help him, he didn't care. Never before had he let a woman manipulate him like this. Never before had he liked it so damn much.

"Good."

He brought his other hand to her waist, and powerfully hauled her against his erection. She gasped. He leaned down to smooth his lips over hers, but not giving in to the kiss.

"Maybe, given the evidence, you might like to do all that again. Over and over," she breathed against his mouth.

"Fuck yes." With that he snaked both his arms around her waist fully and plunged his tongue inside her. His heart pounded in his chest feeling her tongue slide against his, and her full breasts pressed against his chest. She brought her arms up and snaked them around his neck. He slid a hand down to caress her beautifully rounded behind. Her moan escaped into his mouth.

She fit so well against him. It would feel even better without the barrier of clothing between them. He pulled back and saw the clear longing in her eyes.

He yanked on his tie and whipped it off his neck. She reached up and went to work on his shirt buttons. He toed off his shoes and shucked his pants, adding it to the pile. Then he reached for her tank. His movements were so fast, he nearly ripped the top. She stripped off her shorts, and in a bold move, she jumped in his arms, straddling his waist. He grabbed her tight and met her lips as they crashed down on his.

"Cole, I want you bad. I haven't stopped thinking about Saturday."

He carried her into the bedroom and laid her on her queen-size bed. He flicked her bra off and flung it across the room. Then brought his mouth to her dusty pink, eager nipples. He licked, sucked and tugged with his teeth, and tortured the other with his forefinger and thumb.

"Cole—" she breathed as she bowed her back off the bed.

He rose from the bed, jerked off his socks and his briefs. Then hooked his fingers in her thong and dragged it down her legs. It felt like Christmas, unwrapping his gorgeous Alex. Plump breasts begged for sucking and a creamy naked pussy awaiting his tongue.

He knew what to do next. He knelt on the floor, grabbed her waist and tugged her toward him.

"Ah," she screeched.

He spread her thighs, and slid his hands to her core, gently parting her with his fingers. He blew a warm breath against her. Her hips gave an uncontrolled jump. Then he brought his mouth to her sweet deliciousness and slowly licked from her center to her hot little button.

She arched her back again, and he noticed she grabbed the covers causing her knuckles to whiten. He worked her clit slowly and gently, but she wasn't having any of it. She extended her arms and held his head right where she wanted him. Her breath came more quickly as she rocked against his mouth. Her long, low moan filled the room.

He slipped two fingers in her while he continued his assault.

"Oh," she moaned. She writhed on the bed. He heard "Oh" again.

He increased the speed of his fingers pumping into her. And moments later she cried out his name in pure pleasure. Sweet cream squirted across his tongue.

He rose over her after she came down. She opened her eyes to meet his, grabbed his face and pulled it down to meet hers for a heated, appreciative kiss.

"Your turn," she proclaimed and tipped their bodies over to top him.

"Whoa," he said in surprise.

"Um, one thing first." Then she reached down, taking a hold of his large, beautiful erection, and straddling him, she carefully lowered herself over him. They both moaned, and she closed her eyes and let her head fall back, savoring the exquisite sensation.

"Wait, Alex!" he practically threw her off. "I need a condom."

"Shh," she whispered as she slithered down his body. Leaving a trail of kisses on his delectable body, she made her way to his rock-hard penis. She glanced at him, giving him a reassuring smile.

She had condoms, but she had to taste him. Had to pleasure him like he pleasured her. She wrapped her fingers around him, closed her lips around the head of his cock and ran her tongue in his slit. His hips flexed.

She licked him down the underside, and closing her lips over him, sucked while pulling back to the tip. She picked up a subtle taste of herself on him.

"Shit, Alex."

She continued going up and down his shaft until he flexed in tempo with her movements. He grabbed her head and held her as he pumped. He touched the back of her throat, but she still couldn't take him all. She sucked him harder and loved the groan he let out. His eyes closed. With little delay, he climaxed and let go in her mouth. She savored the salty-sweet mixture and swallowed him entirely.

He took a hold of her shoulders, still panting and brought her to his chest. "Christ, Alex. That was amazing."

She rested her cheek on his warm chest and listened to his heart pounding in her ear. He wrapped his arms around her torso and kissed the top of her head.

"I'm glad you liked it," she murmured, and a feeling of utter contentment fell over her. It felt right being with Cole. In his arms. She could think of nothing better.

"So you're my hag?" he broke the silence.

She lifted her head, meeting his gaze, and smiled. "Yes, I am."

His lips pursed pulling his lips to the side. "Alright. I'm good with that. Now, how about some dinner wench."

She pushed back, lifting herself off him more. "Don't press your luck, bub."

A slow, sexy smile came across his face. "Alright." He reached a hand up, cupped the back of her head, and brought her lips to his for a soft, lingering kiss. After a moment, "Do you have anything we can make for dinner that I can help you with, sunshine?" he said.

That's better. "How does taco salad sound?"

"Sounds great."

They got up from the bed, she scampered to the great room and threw on her tank and shorts, sans undergarments. He used the bathroom and then joined her in the kitchen. She put him to grate cheese and dice tomatoes while she browned the ground beef. After several minutes, dinner ready, he set the table for them and pulled out a chair.

"You want a beer?" she called to him.

"Please."

She brought over two light beers and took the seat next to him. He took off both bottle caps, handed her one and held up the other. "To gay men, and their very sexy Fag Hags."

She chuckled. "Cheers," they clanked their bottles.

They dug in because, by appearances, they were both famished. Maybe it was the sex, she thought.

"What have you been doing around here?" he asked catching a view of her little toolbox against the wall.

"I'm hanging pictures and the drapes against that big wall of windows."

"I can help you with that," he said.

"Thank you. It's getting late now. Maybe later this week," she said with a smile.

"Just let me know."

They continued to eat and chat. He asked her about LA and her acting jobs there. She told him about her new agent and how excited she was about Paul. Then, she switched gears.

"What's Lauren doing in Paris?"

"Apparently, we had an aunt, my mother's only sister, who died recently. Lauren was supposed to go to handle the estate."

Her hand lay over Cole's saying "I'm sorry."

His lips curved slightly. "Thanks, but I don't remember her. She lived in Paris most of the time when I was young. I guess she never got married, never had kids, so whatever remains is coming to us."

Her eyebrows rose. "Wow. Nice. So, what made you decide to fill in for your sister at the spa?"

The pause mid-bite was almost imperceptible, but Alex caught it out of the corner of her eye.

Cole finished his bite, set down his fork and took a sip of beer. "Well, Lauren somehow thought I'd be most qualified. I don't know about that. I think it's more that she trusts me to take care of things while she's away." He shrugged a shoulder.

Alex nodded. "Hmm. You guys are pretty close, huh?"

Cole glanced down at his bowl. The silence hung between them. He seemed to wrestle with what he wanted to tell her.

"The death of my parents tore my world apart. One minute they were there, and the next minute they were gone. Forever. It was just Lauren and me. We moved in with my aunt and uncle afterward." He looked up and faced her. "They tried to keep everything as normal as they possibly could, but it would never be the same again for us. I think Lauren handled it better, but . . . I don't know. Life didn't seem as fun or interesting or colorful afterward."

She nodded.

"I think because we lost our parents when we were young, we've always been there for each other. Going through something like that, I suppose, either makes you or breaks you. For us, it made us stronger. We trust each other completely."

He took another sip of beer. "Lauren's due back in a few weeks. She met someone."

She raised her head. "Yeah?"

Cole pursed his lips. "Yeah, some French guy."

"And you don't like that."

"I don't know." He let out a puff of air. "I suppose. I just don't understand how she can go bat-shit over a guy after less than two weeks."

Alex bit her lips together and looked down at her bowl moving the remaining food around.

Noticing her quiet, he asked, "What?"

She licked her lips and raised her head to look at him. "I suppose I can relate to your sister."

She said too much. *Me and my big mouth.* With the unquestionable need to put distance between her and Cole, she got up and walked to the fridge. "Can I get you another beer?"

"Sure." He swallowed his last bite and pushed his bowl back. She handed him a beer and popped her own open for a swig. Then she picked up the bowls and placed them in the sink.

Cole rose and wandered to the wall of windows to check out the night view.

"Thanks for dinner," he said casually.

"You're welcome," she made her way past the sofa to stand beside him. Completely dark now, the lights of the city illuminated the landscape. Close buildings blocked some of their sight, but tall skyscrapers were still visible in the distance.

"You have a pretty cool view," he noticed. "Care if I turn off these lights?" he nodded his head toward the apartment.

She tilted her head. "Sure, go ahead."

He hit the lights, and the apartment went black. He meandered back toward her and stood behind her, instead of at her side.

"Better," he said low in her ear.

Oh shit. He had something planned. She licked her lips and tried to focus on something—anything— out the window. He brushed her hair off to one side and placed a kiss just under her ear. Then another. And another.

She heard her breathing get louder as his warm hands smoothed down her back and then up under her shirt. She placed her hands on the windows to help keep her balance.

His hands slowly smoothed over the skin on her back, her waist and to her belly.

"Yeah, I guess I can understand what my sister might be feeling too," was all he said as he kissed and licked her neck while his hands moved over her swelling breasts.

She dropped her head to the side, relishing his kisses and licks on her neck.

He massaged, twisted, and played with her beaded nipples. She moaned and arched into his hands.

"Cole," she breathed.

He slowly pushed her tank up and over her breasts to gain better access. She should be concerned about flashing half the city. All right, that might be a tad over-exaggerated. She let herself get caught up in the moment. Cole's hot breath on her neck and his wonderfully hot hands cupped and massaged her breasts. The wetness between her thighs grew with every passing moment.

"Let me have you, Alex. Right here. Right now."

"Yes." Her words, barely above a whisper.

Geez! She was an exhibitionist. First outside at her parents' farm. Granted, the neighbors were certainly not close enough to see anything even if they were awake. And now, in front of her huge window in her third-story apartment.

His expert hands made their way down to her cut-offs, undoing the button and fly. Then his big hands slid over her hips and pushed her shorts down her legs.

It was official—she flashed the internationally known New York City. She must have lost all common sense. Or she was too much in lust to think clearly.

"Step out of your shorts and spread your legs for me," he spoke in her ear.

She did as he bid. Gingerly he smoothed her wet folds and clitoris with his strong fingers. A deep moan escaped her throat, and her head fell forward.

"So wet, Alex. You feel amazing."

She felt him move one hand to free his pants, then heard rustling and the clear sound of a condom wrapper. Such a boy scout.

His fingers worked in concert to spread her lips and slowly he pushed passed her tight opening.

"Oh—" The sensation between her legs as she and Cole connected was nothing like she'd ever experienced before. She arched her back to give him better access. His hips slowly gyrated in and out in a methodical rhythm. He brought one hand across her torso to below a breast, his other massaged her clit with just the right amount of pressure.

"Cole, that feels so good," she panted out.

"I could stay inside you all day and night, Alex." His movements stayed controlled allowing her climax to build steadily.

"Ah—" flew out of her mouth, her release teetering on the edge.

He froze. "No, Alex. Wait for a bigger one. Not the first, not the second. Wait for the third. Build it."

Holy shit. How he understood the woman's body. She could do that—or rather would do that. When she was by herself, she could bypass the smaller orgasms, knowing she could bring herself to something bigger. Well, touching herself versus a hunk of a man whispering in her ear, his delicious penis buried inside her while massaging her just-so were two completely different things.

She breathed deeply, and he continued. Again he exercised slow, deliberate control.

"Wider, Alex," he breathed in her ear.

She spread her legs wide, but to her surprise his finger only glossed over her clit with half the pressure of before. Her eyes closed.

"Cole—" was all she could manage. She let her head loll forward between her slightly shaky arms and panted desperately.

"Let me love your body, Alex," he growled out as if he was on the very edge he brought her too.

Slowly, rhythmically he moved inside her, picking up speed.

"Ah," she moaned.

With both hands gripping her hips, he thrust deeper and deeper. Simultaneously, she pushed against the window to counterthrust. Four more thrusts. She exploded with him, shuttered and screamed out his name, not even remembering her own.

After a few brief moments, they collapsed to the floor in a pile of hot, sweaty contented bodies. Satiated by the most astounding orgasms to ever take place in the Northern Hemisphere.

"God, Cole. That was incredible."

Feeling his chest rise and fall, he said in a low tone, "We are."

He was right, and hearing him say it made her feel on top of the world. He made her feel like she was all that mattered to him.

He kissed Alex goodnight at her backdoor before heading downstairs to return to his place. He wanted to stay, she'd asked him to, but he couldn't. The sex between them was phenomenal. He meant what he said—he could fuck her all day and all night. Cole had his share of women, and most of the time sex between them had been satisfying. But truthfully, he never *needed* them longer than a few weeks. They would go out a few times, roll around a few, but then an unfathomable need to pull away rode him hard. It felt like claustrophobia. He never came close to feeling that with Alex. It was the exact opposite—he couldn't get enough of her.

As he strolled down the sidewalk toward his place, he scratched the side of his head and smoothed his hair. He wondered. Why hadn't he told Alex the whole story about his aunt's estate? Why hadn't he told her it was valued at three million dollars? And did she understand how careful they would have to be? If it got out that he was *with* a woman, the shit would hit the fan. He shook his head. *Don't think about it.*

CHAPTER SIXTEEN

ALEX WAS MAKING salmon for dinner when her cell rang. She'd lucked out finding fresh Alaskan salmon on sale.

She read the name on the screen and smiled.

"Hey, Aidan. What's up?"

"You don't have to work tonight, do you?"

"No. Why do you ask?" she opened her toaster oven and slid the salmon in.

"You up for some karaoke?"

She stopped in her tracks. "Seriously?"

"Yeah. Jade knows a place not far from here. Apparently it's real fun. I think I'll call Cole too."

She didn't have anything planned, which was pathetic, but this would get her out of the house. Not to mention, any reason to see Cole worked great for her.

"Okay. What time?"

"Meet us at my place at eight. It won't be a late night."

"Okay, see you then," she hung up the phone.

A little after eight Aidan, Jade, Cole and Alex walked into the happening karaoke bar. They all followed Jade since she was the only one who had been there before.

"Hey, Jack," she called and waved to the bartender, who waved back.

Jade wend through the crowd to find an empty table stashed against the wall. All the chairs had been hijacked, but Cole and Aidan were able to scrounge up four chairs and carry them over. It looked to be a pretty decent set-up because they had a good view of the stage.

"The bridge and tunnel crowd is out tonight," Jade said as her eyes scanned the busy place. She was right. They were lucky to have found a place to sit considering most everyone had to stand. Alex noticed the pack that gathered around the bar waiting to order drinks.

The waitress didn't take long to stop by and collect their drink orders.

"So, Alex, how's work going for you? Acting, that is?" Jade asked her.

"I've gone on a few calls, just waiting to hear back. My agent has a few auditions lined up for me next week and the following week too. It's starting slow, but it'll pick up."

"I'm sure it will," she said as the corners of her mouth curved.

The waitress returned with their drinks, two for everyone.

"What's this?" Aidan asked tugging at his ear.

"Two-for-one night. And," she slipped a stapled booklet of paper out of her apron, "here's the song selections. Just enter your name and your song in either the tablet at the bar or the stage."

Jade grabbed the booklet, eyes wide, and she started flipping through the pages. Aidan placed his arm over the back of her chair and leaned in to glance over her shoulder.

Without even looking up, she asked, "Do you karaoke, Alex?"

Aidan brought his head up, caught Alex's gaze and smiled.

"A little," Alex said.

Cole hadn't said much all night. She suspected he didn't want to slip up and say something uncharacteristic and give himself away, but when he glanced over at her, a twinkle of amusement shone in his eyes.

"I gotta see this," he murmured.

Jade spun the booklet over to Alex. "I got my song. Your turn," and with that she rose to go enter her song selection.

Alex flipped open the book and read the multitude of songs.

"Pick out something to wail, Alex," Aidan said as he reclined in his chair.

"Something to wail, huh?" she muttered. Then to her surprise she gleaned just the song she could let loose on. The corners of her mouth rose marginally. She pushed back the chair and stood to go enter her song.

Jade's name was announced by the DJ. She happily jumped up, gulped the last of her drink and wend her way to the stage. She sang "Come on Over" by Christina Aguilera. She seemed to thoroughly enjoy herself as she danced around the stage. At one point, she waved a come-hither finger toward Aidan and gave him a wink. She certainly energized the crowd. Aidan, Cole and Alex stood for their applause.

Next, a boyfriend-girlfriend duo sang a drippy love song. They were silly and, despite being off-key a few times, they appeared to satisfy the crowd.

The DJ called Alex's name right after. She followed Jade's suit, took a big swig of her whiskey sour and grabbed the mic, licked her lips, and got ready for a little fun. She picked "Sweet Nothing" by Calvin Harris because she loved it, *and* she knew the song like the back of her hand. She also knew the lyrics started one beat after the music. She inhaled deeply, watched the TV screen change in front of her and let out the first note right on cue.

She loved this song, and as the tempo increased, so did her performance and animation. Not needing to look at the screen for the lyrics, she watched the audience.

They seemed captivated.

Aidan smiled like a proud brother. Growing up, he used to tease her about singing around the house and in the shower. Her eyes traveled to Jade, who seemed to be singing along, then moved on to Cole, who held his stare on her intently. She almost believed she was the only person in the room for him.

At the song's crescendo, she dropped to her knees and let her torso fall forward. She poured herself into the song as if it were the last song she'd ever sing. Perhaps a bit dramatic, but she was an actress after all.

When she finished, the crowd went crazy with applause, hoots, and hollers. She stood, smiled and blotted her upper lip. She handed the mic to the DJ who called for another round of applause. Her heart continued a wild beat as she returned to the table.

"Holy shit. You've got great pipes, girl," Jade exclaimed wearing a wide smile.

"Good job, sis." Aidan leaned forward to plant a kiss on her cheek.

She then turned to face Cole, who gave her a smile that didn't touch his eyes. They had the same penetrating, intense look she saw weeks ago at Aidan's. They had turned a deep green and appeared dark as if heat resonated from within.

"Well done," he said in a deep, sexy voice as he reached to pull out the chair for her, not breaking his fix on her.

Oh shit. The sound that came out of Cole's mouth flowed over her like hot, liquid chocolate. Alex stilled and her heart skipped a beat. Something hot and wild had roused in Cole that singed the outer protective shell on Alex. It felt as if Cole could look right through to her core.

Her mouth gaped. She turned away, closed her mouth and inhaled through her nose. She couldn't help the thoughts of her and Cole that flashed through her mind. She squirmed in her seat as she finished her drink.

The waitress swung back around to take orders, but Alex requested only water. She *wanted* something stronger, but thought the wiser.

The group watched the entertainment, and the crowd as it got more animated and loud. Alex had the impression several of the loudest people were passed their drinking limits.

"How about we head out, guys? I've got work in the morning," Jade proclaimed.

"Great idea." Cole stood and took Alex's hand as she rose.

What?

Perhaps realizing what he'd done, he dropped it almost immediately. The warmth he left in her hand dissipated quickly, and she missed it. She had a brief glimpse of what it might be like to be Cole's girlfriend, and she loved it.

Outside, darkness fell and the street crowd had thinned.

"Okay, we'll catch you later," Aidan said as he hugged Alex and fist bumped Cole.

Jade gave her a hug too.

"Goodnight. Thanks for coming out." They crossed the street, heading to Jade's place.

Cole and Alex walked for several minutes not saying much, and when they were to turn left toward her apartment, he said, "No. My place."

She contained her surprise.

"Okay." That's when she knew for certain—he had something in mind.

He unlocked his apartment and held the door open for her. As Cole flipped on a light, she let her gaze travel the space. She could see Lauren's touch— the flowing linen drapes, the colorful pillows, and a few live plants.

"Nice place, Cole."

He acted like he didn't hear her. "Tell me about that song you sang tonight."

She drew her eyebrows together. "What about it? I like it, so I decided to sing it."

He unbuttoned the cuffs of his dark shirt and started to roll them up several times. "You seemed to know the words very well."

She kept an eye on his movements, because she was beyond intrigued. "I . . . that's what happens when you like a song. You learn the words."

He slowly walked toward her. She swallowed and backed up. He stepped forward and she backed up until her calves hit the sofa.

"Sit," he said.

He slid her purse off her shoulder and bending at the knees, he reached down and removed her sandals. Each movement deliberate.

He brought his eyes back to her. "Of all the songs you could sing, you sang 'Sweet Nothing'?"

She smoothed her lips together. Her heart raced, like a rabbit on the chase. But God, did she love the chase with Cole.

"Yes," her voice so small.

He placed both hands to each side of her on the sofa and brought his face inches from hers, forcing her to lean back just to keep eye contact.

In a whisper, he said, "Is that what you think you get from me, Alexandra? Sweet nothing?"

She bit back a smile. "What? No," she said nearly breathless.

She might be nervous, but she was also insanely curious about what he had planned for her, she couldn't help to stay planted.

He blew a breath on her neck, and she shivered.

"Hmm," as if he had something more to say. Instead, his hands went to her pants, undoing the button and zipper. He pulled back and commanded, "Lift."

She lifted her hips because she couldn't clearly think of a good reason not to. He slid her jeans down her legs and tossed them. He knelt in between her legs and slid his hands up her thighs. Slowly caressing but never smiling as he looked at her.

His ministrations sent a tremor up through her body. Her breasts felt heavy, and her nipples puckered with his intense stare.

"What are you wearing, Alexandra? A thong?"

She nodded.

"Let me see." He shuffled on the carpet to the side. "Lay on this coffee table."

What? She swallowed hard. She scooted to the edge of the sofa, dropped to her knees and laid her belly on the table. It felt cold, although perhaps it was just because she was so warm.

He took his large hand and caressed her bare behind.

"I love these black lacy panties on you, so much that—" Then he brought his hand back and came down in a rapid swat on her ass. She yelped. "I won't rip them off you."

The smack was a fine line between pain and pleasure. He caressed her skin, but she had the distinct feeling he wasn't through.

Another smack, followed by a caress. She let out a screech.

"I love to have my hands on your ass, doing a lot of nothing." He enunciated the last word.

Another smack and this time the contact was directly over her pussy.

"Ohh," she moaned.

He slapped her derriere again letting his fingers stroke her core and panties, wet from the pleasure he brought to the surface. Then he pushed her t-shirt up higher on her torso.

"This lovely thong is soaked from, nothing. I think we should take it off." He reached both hands to the sides, grabbed the fabric and slid it down past her ass to her knees.

"Alex," he leaned over and whispered in her ear while he continued to caress her behind, "you have an excellent voice." *Swat!* "I shouldn't have been surprised coming from that beautiful mouth of yours." Swat again, and her moan was the loudest yet.

Oh, God. Could she come from this? The intensity of the movement was both foreign and exciting. He caressed her core again with his talented fingers.

With his free hand, he swept her hair aside to kiss and lick her neck. At the same time, he slowly slid his index finger inside her aching channel.

"Oh, look how wet you are from doing . . . nothing."

Then he added another long finger, stroking her core, turning and twisting. She gripped the edge of the table, her orgasm close.

"Do you like this Alexandra?" he breathed in her ear.

"Yes," she panted.

"Is this nothing? Or is this something?"

Her chest swelled. "Something, Cole." Her breath fogged a spot on the table. "Everything, Cole. Everything."

He pushed in one more finger and pumped causing her to tremble. The orgasm ripped through her like wildfire. Astonishing. She screamed out his name.

Cole swiftly whipped off his shirt, undid his pants and donned a rubber. The sight of Alex spread over his coffee table with her bare pink ass in the air was nothing short of spectacular. He felt an almost excruciating ache to get inside her.

He lifted her off the table, spun her around, pulled her flush against him, and plunged his lips down on hers. His tongue drove into her sexy mouth. He kissed her deeply as she moaned in his mouth. Their tongues tangled.

He pulled back long enough to yank her t-shirt over her head and on the way back down, flipped the clasp on her bra and flung it aside. Then he laid her down on her back between the coffee table and the sofa, his cock positioned between her legs. Their fingers interlaced above her head when he kissed her passionately, desperately.

"Knees up," he breathed against her lips.

She brought her knees up, which opened her easily for him to slide in. With a controlled flex in his hips, he slid his cock into her warm center. She arched, and he groaned audibly.

"Cole," she breathed.

"Alex, look at me." She opened her eyes to see him. "You were incredible tonight. I felt proud to see you up there. I felt good hearing you sing like that. Now, I want to make you feel good." He laid one last kiss on her as he continued to pump steadily. Letting go of her hands, he said, "Keep them there, sunshine."

Her hands spread out over her head, as he arched his torso and brought his lips to her primed, pink nipples. He took one nipple and tenderly sucked and licked. He sucked the underside of her creamy breast before going to the other one, repeating the treatment. He knew he might have marked her, not that he was concerned. He smiled. Every time she saw the hickeys, she would think of him.

He took one nipple and sucked harder. She gasped. He pumped faster and laved her nipple, giving it a little nibble.

"Unh!" Her body jolted.

Her hips rose and began a dance in sync with his thrusts.

"Cole," she moaned again. "Don't stop."

"Never. Let me feel you milk me. Come, sunshine."

It didn't take long before she did. She reached her arms around his neck, pulled him down to her and moaned into his mouth as their hips moved wildly together. Then he pulled away and bowed his back for the most powerful orgasm he ever had. Brief moments later he collapsed over her chest and panted into her shoulder.

"Holy cow." Her chest rose and fell with her labored breathing. "Where did that come from?" He knew she was referring to their electrified foreplay.

"You. I told you. You make me crazy."

A beautiful slow smile came over her kiss-swollen red lips.

"Good," she reached her hands to his cheeks, stroking his face as she pulled up and placed a kiss on his lips. "It's getting late. You have to work in the morning. I should head home," she carefully rose to her knees as she gathered her garments strewn about the floor.

His mouth opened then closed. As he watched her, his lips pressed in a slight grimace.

"I'd ask you to stay, but I can't."

She looked his way and shrugged. The twinkle in her eyes seemed to dissolve. "I know. Someone could see me leaving in the morning. Someday soon, though, I hope."

He rose to stand beside her and brought her still naked body against his. "Definitely," he placed a gentle kiss on her lips, backed off a fraction, to get a close look into her beautiful brown eyes. "I'll get dressed and walk you." Before she could protest, he raised a finger to hush her. "Get dressed."

***

Cole walked her home. They didn't hold hands, but she looped her arm through his, and kissed him on the cheek at her door. The night was unexpectedly good. Karaoke felt exhilarating. She smiled in recollection. She relished having a mic in her hands.

And lest she forget the sex. The sex was hot, passionate and crazy good. Her bottom still tingled. The more Cole got turned on, the more she got turned on. The only thing to make the night perfect would have been spending the night with him, feeling his arms wrapped around her, and his warmth next to her. She sighed.

She stripped for bed, and saw the love bites he left on her breasts, maybe three or four at the most. Being with Cole was always amazing, and when she wasn't with him, she thought of him. She bit down on her lip.

She was falling, and falling hard.

CHAPTER SEVENTEEN

BUSINESS AT THE SPA so far this week was stellar. A few new clients, but more importantly several add-on services sold, thanks to Gretchen and Andrea.

Cole was about to head back to the office for a bite and to email Lauren, when Jessica Fulton sauntered in with, presumably, her brother Bryce. How had he missed that she had an appointment today? He frowned inside while trying to keep a smile on his face.

"Hello, Colton. I know Bryce can't stay, but I really wanted you to meet him," she positively beamed. "Bryce, this is Colton. Colton, this is Bryce."

Becky approached the desk, not realizing Mrs. Fulton might not be ready for her service because she was too busy matchmaking. *Lord.* He felt a single trickle of sweat stream down the back of his neck.

Mrs. Fulton seemed perfectly content on leaving the men alone.

"Hi, Becky." Then turning to Bryce, "Well, I'll just leave you two to chat for a bit. I'll call you later, Bryce." And she and Becky were gone.

"So, my sister tells me you're filling in for your sister while she's away. What do you do?"

"I own a remodeling company."

"Really," he said with a high inflection. "Fascinating."

No, it really isn't.

"Look, Bryce—"

Bryce cut him off when his hand flew up palm-out. "I know how you feel. This whole fix-up scene is not your thing. I couldn't agree more. Been there, done that," he said as he flapped his hand out to the side and rolled his eyes. "But I figure since I'm here now, why don't we trade numbers and at least agree to meet for a drink somewhere soon? I heard of a fabulous place in the East Village we can check out," his eyes look shiny and eager.

Finally, the guy shut up. Cole pressed his lips together.

"What I was going to say is that I can't go out with you. I met someone."

Bryce's shoulders fell. "Oh."

"Yes, and I don't think it would be fair to you or him to be two-timing. I hope you understand."

Bryce's eyes narrowed. "What's his name?"

Crap! "Alex."

"What's he like?"

This was easy. Cole leaned forward, closing the gap a bit. "Touchable brown hair, sparkling brown eyes, kissable soft lips, and an amazing body."

Bryce's eyes softened. "Sounds dreamy."

"Definitely the stuff dreams are made of." *Yes, she was.* Cole straightened and waited for Bryce's next move.

"Well, good luck to you. But if it doesn't work out, give me a call."

"Absolutely. And good luck to you." Cole gave the man a polite smile before he turned and made his way out.

Cole had sailed through that by the skin of his teeth.

He blotted his brow and waved Andrea over to cover the desk as he headed to the back office. His escape for a while.

***

Eric finished wiping down the bar top and walked to the back where Alex loaded the dishwasher. He brought the empty bowls and set them in the sink.

"Hey Alex. Would you mind if I punch out early? I told my cousin I'd drop in on his bachelor party tonight."

She glanced at her watch. "Will it still be going on?"

He grinned. "Yes, unfortunately. If it's anything like his first one, I might make it home when the sun rises." His facial expression changed, showing almost regret. "I'd invite you if it weren't men-only."

"Not a problem." *Really!* "Have a good time. I'll give the bar a once-over. The tabletops still feel sticky. And the band's room needs cleaning. I should be out of here in twenty, thirty minutes tops."

He stepped closer, invading her personal space. "Are you sure? You have mace, right?"

"I'll be fine, Eric," she exhaled and nodded at him. Then, taking her completely by surprise, he wrapped both arms around her and hugged her for what felt like an eternity.

"Ok, call if you need anything. I'm locking the door," he said with an insistent tone in his voice.

"Okay," she said just as insistently back, although she held back the smirk.

She powered on the washer and headed to the bar area to clean and sanitize. She worked in enough bars to know the smell of spilled beer grew foul quickly. She learned a trick to get the place back to like-new. When the tables were finished, she picked up her spray bottle to wipe down the back room when there was a knock at the door.

Who the hell would it be at this late hour?

She peered through the peephole. Cole. Her heart gave a little pitter-pat.

"Hey, you. What are you doing here so late?"

"I came to walk you home." He strolled inside looking gorgeous as ever in his fitted jeans and a simple t-shirt.

"Well, I'm almost done. Just one room left."

Cole glanced around the empty bar. "Where is everyone?"

"They left already."

"Well, shit. I'm really glad I stopped by."

"Don't worry. I planned on taking a cab."

He harrumphed, and she bit back the smile. "Come on back."

"You're wearing a skirt," he said trailing her into the band room.

So? She tipped her head and pinched her brows together. Turning her full attention to Cole, her confusion began to fade as she got a clear look at his darkening eyes. Her heart rate skyrocketed in mere seconds. He stepped in her direction, closing the gap between them.

She held out her hands.

"No. Noo—" She was cut off as he grabbed her wrist and in three strides had her bent over a club chair in the room. Her waist bent right over the top and, to stop the sheer momentum of the movement, she braced her hands on the armrests.

"What the hell's your deal?" she squealed, but smiling at the same time.

Both of his large, warm hands ran slowly up her legs, flat palms sweeping right up the middle of her thighs. They found their way under her skirt and pushed the fabric up to her waist. Her breath quickened; she couldn't utter a word of protest.

"I've fantasized about you in a skirt and what I would do to you," he confessed, his voice low and husky.

His hands slid up to her globes. She heard his groan.

"God, you're beautiful."

She smiled, not that he could see with her head facing down and hair falling all around her face. She sighed as he started a slow, erotic massage of her ass. His thumbs grazed over the fabric of her thong in her crack. He stood and leaned over her, his front to her back. She could feel his arousal, which only amped up her excitement.

He whispered in her ear, "I'm going to have you like this, and it will take every ounce of strength not to shoot you to the other side of the room."

Oh.

He leaned down to kiss, lick and nip at her hips and smooth behind. She was eternally grateful for wearing body lotion every day. Everywhere.

She felt herself getting warmer, and tension built in her sex. He pulled her thong aside and lightly stroked his fingers in between her folds. She felt the swipe of his tongue, up and down. He stopped over her swollen clit to knead it gently. She moaned unabashedly loud. He continued his ministrations and, with his very adept fingers, slowly peeled her panties down her legs. Knowing what he wanted before he asked, she lifted one foot at a time to get free of the garment.

"Spread your legs a little more, sunshine," he asked. She did and heard the rasp of his pants zipper and the ripping of the condom wrapper. She panted. His hands slid up the back of her thighs again making their way to her sex. He slowly slid his finger down her cleft.

"So wet." He continued the slow glide with the back of his hand up her crevice.

Her breath hitched.

His hands swept over her behind, wrapped around her hips to the front, splaying down her lower stomach, he pulled her slightly away from the chair. The touch of his hands, the slow glide, sent tingles throughout her body. His hands moved lower still to her sex until his index fingers reached her clitoris and lips. She couldn't stop her hips pulsating against his fingers.

He leaned over her and placed kisses on the back of her neck and between her shoulder blades. Her arms supported her upper body, as she let her head drop. She could feel his soft tongue run a line over her neck.

She wasn't sure how much longer she could wait to feel him inside her.

He stood upright and separated her lips with his fingers. He bent at the knees slightly, placed his erection at her opening, and slid inside her. They both moaned.

His thrust was fast at first, but then he slowed the pace. She bit her lip. He purposefully pulled back, riding her G-spot, massaging with the bulbous head of his penis.

Oh, dear Lord. His movements gave her *the most* exquisite feeling. She could feel his small, pulsing movements, and his deep, long strokes. Alternating short with long strokes. She moaned from the deep sensation building at her sex.

He curled over her. "You like this, don't you, sunshine?" he whispered in her ear.

The cooing in her ear made her heart swell. Cole filled her on so many levels.

She felt her orgasm gain momentum; she trembled. She savored the burn building deep inside.

"Cole," she breathed.

His rocking continued against her, in and out. He seemed to maintain control, holding on to his own orgasm to let her climax first. Her nerves were on fire. Her fingers clenched the upholstered arms of the chair so tightly they turned white. Finally, her orgasm rocketed with such power she momentarily lost touch with reality. She flung her head back and screamed. His pace quickened, and in just moments, he climaxed ferociously. She barely heard his low sexy masculine groan as he collapsed on top of her. Both of them working to catch their breaths and come back down to earth.

After several short moments, she heard his low voice.

"You're incredible."

"So are you."

From the doorway, Eric witnessed what looked to be an unbelievable sex scene. His eyebrows rose when Alex cried out Cole's name. He might never be able to sit in the chair again without thoughts of how Cole . . .Colton took advantage of *his* Alex.

His nostrils flared, and his jaw ticked as he watched Cole drive into precious Alex. His fists constricted as he quietly backed away from the door and slipped back outside.

***

It was Saturday morning, and Cole had spent the night at her apartment. After Alex locked up Peachy's, he walked her home, and when she asked him to stay, he agreed. That was a first. Despite his reservations, he wanted to be in bed with her, wanted to feel her body curled up next to his. Of course, the clock read six-forty, and Cole was in the bathroom getting himself together to leave. A necessary evil.

Cole stepped out of the bathroom, fully clothed.

"Morning, sunshine."

"Morning. How'd you sleep?" she asked as he leaned over her to kiss her gently on the lips.

"Great. I probably should head out and get ready for work." Admittedly, he felt nervous to be seen leaving her place. He knew he took a risk spending the night with her, so he had a sense of urgency to head out now. He'd use the back door, just as they did coming in last night.

"Sure. Let me get you a cup of coffee for the road," she scampered out of bed and threw on a robe. His eyes tracked her movements. The smooth skin and curves of her naked body beckoned him, but he couldn't afford to be distracted.

As the coffee brewed, Cole noticed Alex seemed lost in thought.

"What are you thinking?"

She lifted her head to meet his eyes. "I was just thinking, maybe we could go out sometime—like just you and me—on a real date."

Was she crazy? He ran a hand through his hair. "Alex, you know I can't do that."

"But Lauren will be back in like a week, right? Surely, it doesn't matter anymore?"

He felt his heart rate escalate, and his face get warm.

"Of course, it still matters. I have to keep this up until she returns, and I am free and clear of the place." He stepped closer and took her hand. "It's not that I don't want to go out with you. You know I do. It's just that there's too much at risk."

"You're right. I'm sorry I brought it up. What's one more week," she gave a small smile.

He lifted her chin with his index finger and placed a slow, gentle kiss on her lips. He let his finger trail down her soft throat. He knew this was hard on her. It was hard on him.

"Be strong, sunshine. Lauren will be back soon."

She nodded and poured him a cup of coffee, and before he walked down the back steps, he gave her a long, languid goodbye kiss.

CHAPTER EIGHTEEN

SHE STARTED missing Cole even before he was gone. She shivered. She fell in love with him. She hadn't planned on it; it just happened. And this *job* was making a relationship with him a challenge.

Stop it, she chided herself. She didn't mean to sound or behave like a spoiled child. The truth was she had never been in love before. She wanted to savor every moment of it.

Her cell phone rang and interrupted her reverie. It was her agent.

"Hi, Paul."

"Hi, Alex. Do you have a moment?"

"Sure. What's up?"

"I've replayed your demo tape, and I'd like to hear you sing in person."

What does he have in mind?

"Okay," she said a little hesitantly.

"I may have a job for you. It's an off-Broadway production that requires singing. Any chance I could hear you sing sometime soon?"

Her heart gave a little jump. "Sure. I can be at your office in an hour." She had a few hours before work.

"Unfortunately, the next few days are not good for me. The good news is we have some time before things get underway. How about we get together Thursday?"

Inspiration hit her like a gift from the talent gods. She knew just what to do to impress him.

"Paul, I have an idea. I work at a bar that hosts live musical acts every night. Why don't you come there Thursday night? I can hop on stage for a number.

"Okay," he said, sounding like he liked the idea. "Text me the address and time."

They said their goodbyes, and she practically flew to the ceiling. This was the chance of a lifetime. Ralph would surely let her sing at the bar. Just one song. She had a few days to practice, make sure the band got the song down and the timing.

Now for what to sing. She stood and paced. She licked her lips and a laugh bubbled up.

Oh, she needed to call Cole. Chances were he was at work. She shot him a quick text instead.

Got a call from my agent. He wants to hear me sing for an off-Broadway production!

Cole replied after a few minutes.

That's great, sunshine. He'll be blown away. Are you working? Come over tonight. I'll make you dinner.

She smiled.

OK. Thanks. I'll be there after 9. XX

Alex paced for a while longer over the adrenaline rush. She could do something classic like Barbra Streisand's version of "Somewhere" or something more contemporary like "Rather Be" by

Clean Bandit or perhaps a little slower like "All Of Me" by John Legend. Her mind raced.

She took a deep breath as her heart thundered in her ears. She had to get ready for work. First things first, she needed Ralph's approval. Once she had that, she'd talk to the band and arrange for rehearsal time. She hopped to the fridge getting the creamer for her coffee and some leftover pizza to munch on.

* * *

Business at the spa kept its usual pace. One more week, Cole thought, and Lauren would be back. He hadn't heard from her as often as he would like, and his concern was growing. He strode to the back office and picked up the phone to dial her cell. It would be afternoon there.

"Hello?" she answered.

"Lauren. It's Cole."

"Hi, Cole. How are you?"

"Never mind that. How are you?" His voice sounded gruffer than he intended, but he didn't care.

"I'm good. Busy. The house is getting some showings, but no offers. I think I found some interesting history that the real estate agent can use, and Andre asked me to come on a business trip with him, so I'm packing right now."

What the hell? She sounded like she hadn't a care in the world or that she wasn't thirty-six hundred miles away.

"Lauren, do you think that's a good idea?"

"Sure. The real estate agent has everything under control. There's not much I can do at this point, and I want to see some of the Continent before coming home."

"Continent?" he almost yelled. "Where the hell are you going?"

"Just Croatia. Andre needs to photograph the Brela Beach. It was listed on Forbes as a Top Ten."

Cole sat back in his chair. He had to admit that sounded pretty cool. "So, when will you be back?"

"Well, I . . . I wanted to talk to you about that. I may go with Andre to Pamplona, Spain for the San Fermin festival."

"The running of the bulls?" He sat forward again, then stood. "When is that?"

"It starts on July sixth."

"Christ, Lauren."

"I know," her voice sounded full of regret. "If you don't want me to go, I'll understand. I haven't even spoken to Regina about staying longer. How is she anyway?"

Cole let out a long low exhale. He knew she wanted to go, but he wanted to get on with his life too.

"She's her usual self. Look, do you mind if I sleep on it. Give it some thought."

"Sure, let's talk later," she said sounding a bit more hopeful. "I'll call you when I get back from Croatia."

"Okay. Be careful, please."

"I will. Love you."

"Love you back," he disconnected the line.

He sat back in the chair, rested his head all the way back, and stared up at the ceiling. *Damn!* He was between a rock and a hard place. Helping his sister meant less time with Alex.

Frankly, he couldn't get Alex out of his mind. A smile spread slow and easy over his lips.

What was it about her? She was sassy and fun, appealing and irresistible. Not to mention beautiful. She brought out something in him, he didn't even recognize. Maybe it was love. Who knew? But he felt certain he wanted to explore it further.

Cole was thinking about the menu for the night's dinner--he wanted something special for Alex—when Regina stormed into the spa five minutes after closing.

"You, get out," she said pointing at Gretchen. "You, out," this time to Becky.

"Regina, you mind telling me what is going on," Cole called to her as he quickly strode to the reception area from the back office.

She glared, ready to shoot daggers at him. He had a feeling this was something a little white lie wouldn't fix.

"Ladies, Regina and I need to speak. Please gather your things. We can clean up on Monday." The girls scurried like sugar ants while Regina stomped to the back office.

Oh brother, what's got her in a tizzy, he thought. Cole entered the office and closed the door behind him. She flung her arm out, flapping an envelope in front of his face. Too close in fact, he had to lean back several inches.

"Look at what arrived at my office today?" she seethed, nostrils flaring and sweat beads gathering on her upper lip.

He reached for the envelope and read the typed letter inside. It was short and to the point:

Do you know that one of your employees who is acting gay for his job is in fact NOT gay? Colton Knight is his name.

Holy shit!

He looked at the envelope again. "Where did you get this?"

"It was couriered over today. But that doesn't matter. Are you gay, you conniving little weasel?"

"Regina, there is no need for name calling. I can explain everything. Please have a seat," he kept his voice level in order to calm her when in actuality his heart slammed against his chest. Adrenaline coursed through his veins.

"Fuck, no! I'm not going to sit down. Do you have any idea what you've done? My lawyers are feverishly coming up with a plan to mitigate the damage you've created. Who knows what this will cost me? Or the spa? Our reputation . . . my reputation might be forever tarnished. Who the fuck do you think you're playing with?"

He stood frozen in place, his legs planted wide. He ran a hand over the back of his neck. What the hell had he done? Who knew? Who the fuck sent Regina that note?

"I need your sister to get her ass back here because your ass is fired. What was going through that pea-brain of yours to think this stunt would work? Are you out of your mind?"

I was.

"Where is your sister? How come I can't get a hold of her?" she said still screaming, which was now starting to bring on a ringing in his ears. Or maybe that was the racing blood he heard.

"You called Lauren?"

"Of course I did. I blame her too! Where is she?"

"On her way to Croatia."

"Croatia!" Regina's face turned a red color that had Cole thinking she'd have a stroke if she didn't calm down.

"She'll land soon. I'll get a hold of her."

"The fuck you will. You're getting your ass out of my spa right now, and you better hope like hell I never see your face again."

At that moment, the office door opened to reveal a burly, wide man standing in the doorway, hands clasped in front of him, his eyes trained on Cole. He didn't utter a word. Cole knew that was his escort out of the place.

He gathered what very few things he had, and turned to face Regina, giving it one last try.

"Regina, if you could just let me explain."

"OUT!" she screamed at the top of her lungs, even the security guy flinched.

Cole's blood boiled as he rode the elevator down to the ground floor. Who the hell did this? Very few people knew the truth—Lauren, Ace, and Alex. That was it. There was no one else. His teeth clenched so hard the enamel could wear off.

Since he hadn't been seen with anyone except Alex, he honed in on that as the catalyst for the letter. But when he and Alex were together in public, it was all very platonic. Nothing suspect in their behavior. Right? Cole shook his head and cursed again.

The longer he thought about it, the madder he got. He clenched his fists. The sense of betrayal bore down on him with such intensity. Lauren was counting on him. *Goddammit!* How could Alex do something like this? How?

CHAPTER NINETEEN

ALEX PUNCHED out and gathered her things from a locker. It'd been a good day for tips—a good day overall—but she'd been looking forward to seeing Cole the most. Tonight would be the first time he cooked for her. She smiled picturing such a manly man, apron tied on, sauce spattered about, and pots piled in the sink ready to topple over. She chuckled. Even if he wasn't a good cook, she didn't care. That wouldn't change how she felt about him.

She walked out the front door and turned left to head to his place. She came up short when she caught a glimpse of him waiting, leaning against a building two doors up. Her heart ratcheted slightly seeing him in his denim blue jeans and kohl t-shirt. His hands in his pockets showed off his forearms and biceps, and Alex couldn't wait to run her hands over them.

"Hey, stranger. How's it going?"

He'd been looking down, and only just then did he raise his head to meet her gaze. There was something off tonight. The baby-fine hairs at the back of her neck stood on end.

She approached slowly.

"Is everything alright?" she said in a low voice. She reached her hand to touch his arm, and ignored the pit that developed in her stomach.

"Something happened today. Regina knows I'm not gay," his voice low as he worked his jaw.

Crap!

"Cole, I didn't say anything." She wanted to step back, but she held her ground.

Ignoring her statement, he continued. "I've now been fired, and I don't know where this leaves Lauren. She was counting on me," his head shook from side to side. "You pushed for this." He lifted his head, and his dark eyes locked on hers.

"What?" The blood behind her ears roared, and she was pretty sure her face was void of any color.

"Four short weeks," he murmured as he ran a hand through his hair. "I need some time, Alex. I need to talk to Lauren. Come up with a plan. Figure out what the hell I'm going to do." He squinted his eyes and scraped his hand down his face.

What? She bit her lip and stepped back giving herself distance from the tension rolling off him.

"Cole, I didn't do anything. Please, let's talk about this," she pleaded. Pricks of pain stung the back of her eyes, but she forced the tears to stay.

"There's nothing to discuss." He pulled himself off the wall and stalked off in the opposite direction, leaving her standing alone on the sidewalk, wondering what the hell just happened.

After several beats, she took off, jogging up behind him.

"Wait! Cole," she called after him.

He stopped abruptly and spun around to face her. She nearly slammed into him. He held up his hand in front of her face and exhaled audibly.

"Don't, Alex. I need some space," he ground out. Then he turned his back and proceeded down the sidewalk.

Alex watched him walk away. Her heart sank. The suffocating dread rose in her throat. He blamed her. She wrapped her arms around her belly in self-preservation.

Tears streamed down her cheeks. She was paralyzed, but forced herself to walk home. She realized after a few blocks her chest had tightened, and she found it hard to breathe. *Just make it home before you lose it.*

Ten minutes later, she climbed the stairs to her apartment. She locked the door behind her, fled to her bedroom and buried her face in a pillow before the howl could escape. She convulsed in sobs of anguish. She didn't know what happened, except evidently word got back to his boss that he was straight, and he'd been fired. But it wasn't her. Regardless, he blamed her for being the one to start their relationship.

With her nose buried in the bed and pillows, she could smell Cole. He slept with her last night. Would that have been the last time? The last time he'd be in her bed? The last time they'd make love?

Tears started anew. Why would he think she'd do something that intentionally sneaky and underhanded? Why didn't he trust her?

She sobbed so hard she cried herself to sleep.

***

Ralph had eagerly agreed to let Alex sing a song with the band. He told her *sing as much as you want*, but one song would be all she could muster. She practiced with the band during the day and worked at night. She also had someone to work the spotlight for added effect. Some practices went well, and some were a struggle to get through. Thoughts of Cole continued to crowd her mind.

She asked Ralph to put her on the schedule every day of the week as well. The more she worked, the less time she'd have to think about Cole. Fooling herself that she'd miss him less.

Wednesday, as she got ready for her shift, Eric came into the break room.

"How do you feel about tomorrow night?"

"I think I'm ready," she forced a small smile. She wasn't much in the mood for talking.

"You're going to knock him dead," he said with a nod and a smile.

"Thanks, Eric."

He rubbed his hand up and down her forearm before heading to his locker. Why had he felt he could continue to invade her private space?

Alex closed her locker door and made her way to the bar. She mentally shook her head. Perhaps he thought he was being polite, but for her it felt creepy.

***

Cole got a hold of Lauren, but Regina reached her first. Regina told Lauren she needed to return to New York or be out of a job.

Lauren sounded so upset; it nearly tore his heart out knowing he was responsible. He felt wrought with guilt. He fucked up, and now she'd likely have to cut her trip short. He scrubbed a hand over his face and sighed.

"What are you going to do?" he asked her quietly.

"Hell if I know, Cole. The house hasn't sold, and it needs my attention. But I can't be at two places at once," she sounded agitated. "What happened?"

"I don't know." He sighed. It aggravated the hell out of him that he didn't know who found out and told Regina. "Lauren, I am sorry. I fucked up, and I know it."

"Cole, there's nothing we can do about it now. I need to talk to the real estate agent and come up with a plan." She let out an exasperated sigh. "Just so you know, Regina sent out a letter to the clientele telling them about the situation and how everything was under control since you are no longer working for the spa. Also, she told me she spoke to her attorneys. She's, of course, concerned about lawsuits."

"Shit."

"You got that right." There was a pause on the line. "I need to think on it. You'll probably be picking me up from the airport in a few days."

"Okay. Keep me posted," and they hung up.

Three days since he'd seen Alex. Three fucking long days. He pushed his thumbs into his eyes and rubbed. What was he going to do?

The emotions that welled up inside were foreign to him. Every day he'd argue with himself about whether he should have blamed Alex for the mess he was in.

Every day he racked his brain about who could have sent that letter. Lauren or Ace was out of the question. Bryce or Jessica Fulton, or another spa client seemed unlikely, considering they all believed him to be gay. As did the spa employees.

Deep inside, he knew Alex wouldn't say anything, but what if something slipped? What if she accidentally said something to a co-worker? He let out a curse.

CHAPTER TWENTY

ALEX SHOOK OUT her hands as she paced backstage. She had butterflies in her stomach she hadn't felt since her first real acting job. Chances were part of her nervousness was because of Cole. She missed him terribly. She knew she'd get through this a hell of a lot better if he were in the audience. She looked upward and blinked rapidly. She would not cry—now was *not* the time for an emotional upsurge. She licked her lips and heard the band announce her as a guest singer.

She strolled out to center stage and let the applause fill her, give her much-needed confidence. *My, how different everything looked from this angle.*

"Thank you."

She gave a nod to the bandleader who counted down for the band. She tried to pick a happy or upbeat song, but nothing sounded good. Something about "Another Sad Love Song" by Toni Braxton hit her just right.

The spotlight solely focused on her as she started to sing. Slowly the light illuminated the entire stage, making it in turn easier to see her audience. She spotted her agent. He appeared to have a date with him.

Alex couldn't let him—them—distract her. She focused on hitting every note just as she'd rehearsed this week. As the words washed over her, she heard the emotion in her voice. Emotion about love lost and the memories that still lingered. *Oh God, please help me get through this song.*

It's just. Another. Lonely. Love song.

Crud. That last note may have been a bit too raspy.

Why had she decided to do this? Probably because it felt good, it felt right, but she was with Cole then. Now he was gone, and she was singing this very sad song hoping to get a part in a production she knew little about.

Desperation drove her. She needed to find a way to forget Cole and work would do that. Work always motivated her, distracted her, and fulfilled her.

She finished and took a bow. The smile came naturally across her face as she saw her boss standing with Eric and several other servers, applauding. Her eyes moved to Paul, who smiled and applauded. His date looked rather serious though. A few people stood, and she heard one high-pitched whistle.

She exited the stage left just in a nick of time. All the emotion she poured into that song came out in a rush. The tears flowed down her cheeks and a sob escaped. She slapped a hand over her mouth so as not to be heard.

Her heart ached; she felt empty without Cole. But deep inside she knew this was something he'd have to work out. And she prayed he would.

Suddenly, she felt a hand on her shoulder.

"Are you alright?" Eric asked.

She quickly wiped her eyes and cheeks, and turned.

"Yeah. I'm fine."

He rubbed her arm up and down, and reached his other hand to the other shoulder and pulled her in for a hug. *Okay, that was unexpected.* In fact, she started to feel downright uncomfortable.

He continued to hold her close and then breathed into her ear, "You were incredible tonight. And I just want you to know I'm here for you."

Finally, he released her. She took advantage and stepped back.

"Thanks, Eric. I appreciate it. I need to get out there and see my agent."

"Yeah, sure. Catch you later," he replied.

Paul and his date, Rhonda, arrived at the bar, took a seat and got comfortable at a table facing the stage. They each ordered a drink as the band played a contemporary instrumental song.

The guest singer was announced and a lovely upper-twenty year old brunette walked out on stage. She sang *Another Sad Love Song* with such sincere emotion. It came out soulful, which surprised Rhonda to see in such a young woman.

Paul leaned in to Rhonda, "She's good, don't you think?"

Rhonda turned to face Paul, her lips pursed, "What did you do?"

He only smiled, a glimmer in his eye, and turned his attention back to the stage.

After another minute, Rhonda asked, "She can act too, right?"

"Of course."

The song was almost three-quarters of the way finished when Rhonda murmured, "Shit."

"What?" Paul asked.

Her gaze fixated on the stage, she merely shook her head and continued to watch the show before her.

When the song finished, the singer took a bow and exited the stage. Paul had a smile on his face as he pivoted toward Rhonda.

"So, what do you think?"

"What did you tell her about the production?" Rhonda's voice sounded rough and slightly accusatory.

Paul sat back.

"What? Nothing. You didn't give me a breakdown," he raised his eyebrows.

"Right," she murmured.

"What's wrong?" Paul asked earnestly.

Rhonda turned to face Paul, her mind clearly thinking through something. "The production is about a woman jazz singer who lost her love during World War II."

She looked back at the stage as if the singer would still be there. "And she was magnificent. The emotion in her voice was raw and real and . . . and if she can act, I might very well cast her as the lead."

Paul inhaled sharply. "Rhonda that would be wonderful. As I told you, she went to school here, but her experience is mostly film in LA. She can learn stage. I don't doubt it. She's bright."

"Jesus, Paul, she's got a great voice. I'm surprised she's not a singer. I just hope to hell she can act." And with that Rhonda rose, slammed back the last of her drink, and gave Paul a quick peck on the lips. "I want to see her, tomorrow, in my office." She pivoted on her heels, threw her purse over her shoulder, and headed for the door.

Paul sat back in his chair and grinned. Homerun.

He sipped his drink and waited for Alex to come out. He ordered another drink, and glanced at his watch wondering what was keeping her. He was anxious to share the news. Finally, she strolled out and headed toward his table. Her eyes looked a little glassy and a little red. Like she'd been crying.

"Are you alright?" he asked.

"Yes, fine. Where's your date?"

"Alex, she wasn't exactly my date. She's the casting director for the production I told you about."

Alex gasped, and her eyes rounded as she stared at Paul in shock. "Oh no," she breathed.

He smiled. "No, it's a good thing. She loved you. I mean seriously loved you. She wants to see you tomorrow in her office."

Alex's eyes went wide, and her words caught in her throat. Then her eyes narrowed.

"What if I was horrible?"

"That wouldn't be a problem," he said calmly. "Rhonda and I have known each other a long time." The corners of his lips curved.

He pulled out Rhonda's card from his wallet and slid it over to Alex. "Can you be there tomorrow?"

Alex was awe-struck. What could she say? "Yes," she whispered and nodded.

Paul chuckled again, finished his drink, and he stood. "Good job, kid." Then he pivoted toward the door and left.

Ho-lee cow! A giggle bubbled up. She bolted up to go fetch her purse containing her cell phone. Then she stopped abruptly. She'd wanted desperately to tell Cole, but there was no use. He wouldn't take her call anyway. She sank back down into her chair. The effervescent vibe was gone, just like that.

***

On Friday, Alex arrived at Peachy's earlier than necessary for her shift. She didn't mind; it was better than being home alone with her thoughts.

There was one highlight to the day, she thought. She had her meeting with Rhonda that morning and it felt like they hit it off. A faint smile came across Alex's lips. Rhonda was a fun, sassy, and a straightforward casting director, who seemed to be taken by Alex. Rhonda asked more about her experience, and they arranged a time for a formal audition.

She replayed their conversation in her mind.

"Alex, you've got a great voice. Paul didn't tell me."

"Paul didn't tell me he was bringing you last night."

Rhonda chuckled. "He can be quite a schemer sometimes; I've learned."

Alex sat on a bench in the backroom of the bar and smiled again, but then her thoughts were interrupted by Eric as he walked into the room.

"What's so funny?" he asked.

Oh crap. "Hi. Nothing really. I'm thinking about the meeting I had this morning with the casting director. She saw me sing last night."

"Yeah? That's excellent. I bet she loved you," and then Eric did the strangest thing. He strolled behind her on the way to his locker, he rubbed her back and lean down to kiss the top of her head. What the hell was that about?

She spun around quickly.

"Eric, why do you do that? You act like we're an item, or we've known each other for years."

His eyes went wide like he truly hadn't considered he might be crossing the line.

"Oh, I didn't mean to make you uncomfortable. I just thought you might want someone to lean on considering you broke up with your boyfriend."

His words washed over her like a mudslide. "What? What gives you that idea?" Her eyes narrowed.

"Well, I mean you were crying last night. I assumed it was because you and Cole broke it off. And you can be honest with me—I already know about Cole." He went on so casually, and yet the more he spoke, the hotter her face became. "But I'm here for you, Alex."

She stood; her lips flattened into a straight line.

"I see. So you learned that Cole wasn't gay and sent the letter to his boss at the spa informing her of that?" The adrenaline kicked in, and she could hear her pulse pounding in her ears. She was mere seconds from kneeing the guy in the balls.

"Um . . ."

"Really, Eric. You're going to try and cover now?"

His lips thinned and his nostrils flinched. "No, I'm not going to cover now. Alex, Cole is a liar, and he's no good for you. You shouldn't waste your time going out with a guy like that."

"Oh, and you think I should go out with someone like . . . you? A sneak. Is that right?" She tipped her head, her eyes glared at him.

His face flushed.

She stepped toward him and pointed a finger at his face.

"Stay out of my business and stay out of my life."

She spun around, grabbed her apron off the bench, and slammed the door of her locker shut. The loud clatter gave her some long-overdue satisfaction as she stormed out of the room.

"Sonofabitch! That weasel."

CHAPTER TWENTY-ONE

SATURDAY MORNING. A week since he left Alex and he was done with this shit. He hardly ate, hardly slept. He worked out at the gym like a fiend. He fucked up letting Alex go, and today would be the day to correct it.

He would beg if necessary to get her back. Who knew what the future held with the spa, but that didn't matter much anymore. He didn't want to go another day without her.

He wiped down the steamy mirror in the bathroom and lathered for a shave. So, should he call first, or just show up at her place? In one case, she could hang up on him. The other, she could slam the door in his face.

Option two—he was stronger. If he needed to muscle in, overwhelm her, hold her down, smother her with kisses, and make love to her until she was too weak to fight, he would do it. He would tie her down if necessary and kiss, lick and caress every inch of her. He would make her come with his hand, his mouth, or his cock, whatever it took to bring down her defenses.

Yeah. That was a good plan.

***

Alex looked at her face in the mirror as she wrapped a towel around her wet hair. The woman before her appeared tired and sad. Dark circles under her eyes sent a message of depression. She sighed; another day.

She prayed again last night. She wasn't very religious; she'd easily admit. It's not that she didn't believe in God. She went to church growing up and found it boring like every other child. But she'd never been prayerful, and this past week made her a praying woman.

She wanted Cole back. She knew though that it had to be in his time and on his terms.

As anxious as she was to run to him and tell him Eric was behind the letter, she needed him to come to her on his own. *He* needed to realize she would never intentionally hurt or betray him. He needed to realize he could trust her. Without trust, they had nothing.

She smoothed the lotion on her face when she heard her doorbell. Her heart stopped. It was likely Aidan. Usually, he'd call first. She forced herself not to get her hopes up.

It was not Cole. Not.

She reached to open the door and nearly fainted at the sight of Cole standing at her front door. She was in her bathrobe with a towel on her head. *Shit.*

She opened the door and instinctively crossed her arms.

"Hi," he said softly.

"Hi."

"Do you mind if I come in and talk to you for a while?"

She took a breath. God had answered her prayers, perhaps.

Seeing him before her made her feel excited *and* mad at the same time. She eyed him one last time, then stepped back and swept her arm for him to enter.

He entered slipping his hands into his jeans pockets.

"Do you want to sit?" she asked. Why was she so congenial? She chided herself. Either he begged for forgiveness or his ass was out of here.

He raised his face to meet her eyes. She saw something she never saw before; deep concern, maybe fear.

"No, thanks."

He licked his lips. "Alex, I don't know what to say except that I'm very sorry for what I said last week. You didn't deserve that."

She let the silence hang between them. She wouldn't give him the satisfaction of instant forgiveness. She'd make him work for it.

"I was quick to blame you," he went on, "and I apologize."

She smoothed her lips together and inhaled deeply.

"I believe you are sorry for how you reacted, and for that, I accept your apology. But are you regretful that you blamed me?"

He took a deep breath and nodded.

"Yes. I had no right to be mad. If there is any blame to assign, it goes to me." He ran his fingers through his hair. God, how she missed doing that.

He stepped closer to her. His voice softer, he said, "I'm here to apologize. I was wrong. I screwed up. I think . . ." He pursed his lips. "I think I sometimes have trouble trusting people. But all I can ask is that you give me another chance, Alex."

He reached for her hands, unwrapped them from around her torso and held them in his hands.

"Please give me another chance, Alex." He licked his lips. "I know I have some things to work on, and I'm not saying I won't screw up again. But I will promise you this; I will try to make this up to you. You make me want to try harder." He tipped his head to the side. "I've fallen for you, Alex, and I don't want to be apart for another minute."

Wow! Now that was a pretty decent apology. His eyes were sincere and earnest, and still a little fearful. She recognized that it might be fear of losing her.

"I was hurt, Cole. Then I was mad." She shook her head once. "Mad that you would put all this on me. But at the same time, I prayed. Prayed every day that you would come back. I missed you terribly." She felt the tears well in her eyes.

He released her hands, brought her into his embrace and held her close. For several minutes, the only sound she heard was their breathing and his heartbeat. She missed feeling his arms wrapped around her. A few tears escaped.

He must have heard her sob because he kissed her head and whispered, "Shh."

He placed more kisses on her forehead. He pulled back and wiped her cheeks with his thumbs then he slowly, tenderly kissed her lips. Again, he kissed her and this time she opened her lips to him. He pulled her close and drove his warm tongue to meet hers. She tasted her tears on him. How she missed his kisses.

He broke the kiss to look at her. He took her hands in his.

"Thank for taking a chance on me. For the longest time, I've trusted very few people, Alex, and that stems from old wounds. Wounds that I thought had healed. But that has to change. I can't go through my life thinking people are going to hurt me or leave me or . . ."

"Or die on you."

"That's right." His head gave a little nod. "It's not fair to me or those in my life. It will take time, but I am willing to try."

"Do you trust me?"

He smiled. "Yes. Down to the core."

"Good. Now I have something to tell you. I learned the truth about the letter." She felt Cole stiffen. "Last Friday night when I closed, Eric came back and saw us."

Cole furrowed his brow, then his eyes went wide. "Oh shit."

"I just found out yesterday. Monday, I plan to talk to Ralph about this. Eric is jealous or possessive over me, and I don't know why." She shook her head. Eric was a strange bird. But she knew, based on how Ralph liked to run his business, that this bit of news would not sit well with him.

"That sonofabitch." Cole let go of her hands and stepped back. His face reddened slightly. He spun around, scratched his head, and muttered a curse.

She positioned herself in front of him and reached for his hands.

"Cole, let me handle it. Trust me to handle this," and as she spoke the words, she kept her fix on him.

He stared for a moment and finally spoke, "Okay." He drew her close again. "I do trust you. Besides pounding the guy's face in won't fix things with Regina."

He held her close for several moments. She felt his breath on her face.

"It was weird," he started. "This past week I recalled more memories of my parents than I had in a long time. Flashes of images, you know? My dad and I in the backyard playing catch. My mom and I sitting on the couch reading a Curious George book. I remembered watching my mom cook dinner once; then I remembered seeing you in your kitchen, cooking. An inexplicable feeling came over me, Alex." She heard him sigh. "I'm not making any sense am I?"

She drew back from his grasp and looked deep into his green eyes.

"You are to me. Cole, I'm in love with you, and I'm happy those memories of your parents came back to you."

She rose on her toes, placed her hands around the back of his neck, and kissed him. His sculpted lips played against hers, and he welcomed her tongue with his. His arms brought her snug to his lean broad-shouldered frame. She loved the feel of his body next to hers.

"Take me to the bedroom, Cole," she breathed against his lips.

"I'd love to."

He scooped down to hook one arm under her knees and carried her to the bed. He set her down and lowered himself over her. His lips came back to hers, and his tongue stroked hers. She could kiss him for hours.

Briefly, he broke the kiss to hitch off his knit shirt and toss it on the ground. As he lay back down on his back, he pulled her over him. "Come here."

As she rolled over with him, he pulled open her robe. They both moaned when her bare chest met his—skin to skin. She wove her fingers through his hair and began kissing his jawline and his neck.

His hands slipped beneath her robe to her back and ass. His big warm hands caressed her skin, lighting it on fire. She writhed over him while the wetness at her sex grew.

She wanted to feel Cole inside her again. It had been too long. She sat up straight and shifted to work on his jeans button and zipper. He lifted up his hips, and she drew his pants and briefs down enough to free his cock. She reached to her bedside table and retrieved a condom. Cole grabbed her torso with his hands and brought a breast to his mouth and sucked on a nipple.

"Ah," she moaned.

He continued licking and sucking her nipples. How well he knew what she liked.

"Cole, I need to feel you inside me. Please."

She sat over him and rolled the condom, then as he held her hips, she lowered herself down on him, slowly filling every inch of her. They both moaned.

He pulled her chest on top of his. "Go slow, sunshine. I don't want to rush it."

Oh God. She didn't think she could do that. Her swollen sex ached for release.

As he kissed her deeply, he pushed her legs to straighten over his. The sensation changed inside her. He held her and rocked her over his cock. Her clit rubbed against him. Their slow, steady rock had her panting in his mouth. He did not relent.

"I missed you," he whispered over her lips.

The climax built and Alex couldn't hold back any longer. The tension broke in a rush of relief. She pulled away from Cole's lips for a moment to whimper against his neck, and he continued to rock inside her, letting her tremors subside.

She brought her lips back to his. The slow, deep insinuation of their tongues mirrored the movements of Cole inside her. She felt her muscles tighten again in anticipation of another orgasm. She tried to hold back, but there was no use. She moaned into his mouth.

"Oh God, Cole," she breathed as he continued rocking in her, with her. She felt the wetness—her wetness—smearing all around her sex and his. How many orgasms would he give her before he exploded?

"I want you, Alex. I love you."

"I love you," she replied and with only a few more thrusts, she climaxed yet again.

He gripped her thighs and spread her legs to straddling him. He dove deeper into her as he raised his hips off the mattress and dug his heels in to give him leverage. Mere seconds later, he flexed his head back and let out a long groan and came, calling her name.

She collapsed fully on him, and his arms circled around her. They panted together until he kissed her head and rolled her to the side, pulling out.

"Wow," she smiled at him.

He smiled back in response, a brilliant twinkle in his eyes. He pulled off the condom and wrapped it in a tissue. He removed the last of their clothing and pulled the comforter over their bodies.

They lay together arm in arm for what seemed like an hour. Finally, he broke the silence.

"How did your singing audition go this week?"

She smiled despite the residue of hurt. She would move past this, she knew. Because no one was perfect. She could muster the strength and patience to be there for Cole while he healed. She loved him too much not to be. The time may come when she would need extraordinary support from him, and she didn't doubt he would be there for her.

"It went well. In fact, the casting director asked to see me in her office yesterday morning. We met, and I really like her. The key is, will she like me enough to take a chance?" She shrugged a shoulder. "Anyway, she's going to set up an extended audition for me sometime soon to check out my acting skills," she grinned.

"Alex, I'm sorry I missed it. I bet you were amazing. I know she's gonna love you. What's not to love?" he smirked.

He might not have witnessed her audition, but he would make damn sure something like that never got missed again. He screwed up big time, and he would spend the rest of his life making it up her. Happily.

She chuckled. "Thanks. We'll see," she placed a soft little kiss on his lips.

There was one more thing he needed to share. He trusted Alex and she needed to know it. "There's something I need to tell you. I don't know why I hadn't mentioned it before, but I want you to know."

"Okay."

"I told you Lauren was handling my aunt's estate in Paris. What I didn't tell you is that it's worth about three million dollars. Lauren and I will each get one and a half million dollars."

He expected her to look surprised, but she didn't reveal a thing. She looked straight into his eyes. "I wondered when you were going to tell me."

"What?"

"I knew, Cole. But I also knew you would tell me in your own time, so I didn't say anything."

She knew but didn't say a word or pressure him. His head tilted to the side.

"Thank you." He didn't know what else to say. She just buried herself a little deeper in his heart.

He smiled and leaned forward to give her a long, slow kiss. He would always love kissing Alex. She had a heart of gold.

Breaking the peace, Cole heard his phone ring from inside his jeans pocket lying on the floor. He sighed and begrudgingly picked it up. His body tensed.

"What is it?" Alex raised herself on an elbow.

"It's Regina."

"Oh wow. Get it. Find out what she wants."

He stared at the phone. *Shit.* "Hello?"

"Colton. It's Regina." She spoke in her normal clipped tone. "I need you in my office immediately," and the line went dead.

"What the hell?"

"What is it? What'd she say?"

"She needs to see me in her office now." Cole looked down at the phone and over at Alex, who appeared just as nervous and confused as he felt. He swiped his dry lips with his tongue. *What the hell is this about?*

For the rest of Cole's story, and to read about Lauren, please continue to

Perfect Surrender

By Mia London

Amazon, Barnes & Noble and CreateSpace

Thank you!

ABOUT THE AUTHOR

Mia London loves to write.
After reading fiction for years, she decided it was finally
time to put those images and scenes floating around in
her head down on paper.

She is a huge fan of romance, highly optimistic, and
wildly faithful to the HEA (happily ever after). Her goal
is to create a fantasy you will enjoy with characters you
could love.

She lives in Texas with her attentive, loving, super-
model husband, and perfectly behaved, brilliant
children. Her produce never wilts, there are no weeds in
her flowerbeds and chocolate is her favorite food group.

www.Facebook.com/MiaLondonAuthor
www.MiaLondon.com
Email: mia@mialondon.com